# AIN'T NO KING OF THE Streets

# AIN'T NO KING OF THE Streets

by

## C.L. LOWRY

**CREEDOM PUBLISHING COMPANY**

Published by Creedom Publishing Company

The Cataloging-in-Publication Data is on file at the Library of Congress.

creedom

ISBN: 978-1-946897-19-0

Printed in the United States of America
10 9 8 7 6 5 4 3 2 1

Dear Reader,

Welcome to the captivating series of The Street Kings, where the boundaries of traditional storytelling are deliberately blurred. I want to guide you through a remarkable literary experience that invites you to explore the narrative in an unconventional way.

Within the world of the Street Kings, I have intentionally crafted a novella series of interconnected stories that defy the conventional norms of sequential reading. Each book in the novella series is an independent tale, a self-contained universe brimming with its own characters, mysteries, and adventures. These books are designed to be enjoyed as individual gems, offering a unique and satisfying journey with every read.

Embrace the freedom to dive into the world of the Street Kings at your own pace, without the constraints of a traditional fixed reading order. Feel free to follow your instincts and choose the book that calls out to you. Whether you begin with the Queen of Hearts or venture into the depths of the King of Diamonds first, each entry in the novella series promises a complete and fulfilling narrative experience.

I intend to empower you, the reader, to curate your own path through this literary tapestry. As you navigate through the tales within this series, you will uncover threads that connect the stories in unexpected ways. The choice of the sequence is yours, and I hope you will relish the excitement of piecing together the larger picture as you embark on your journey and prepare for *King of the Streets 2*.

So, heed this disclaimer as an invitation rather than a caution. Embrace the freedom to explore, wander, and be pleasantly surprised by the intricate web of storytelling in each book. With each story, you are embarking on a fresh adventure, a new perspective, and an opportunity to savor the series in a way that resonates uniquely with you.

Thank you for choosing to experience this series in all its unconventionality. Prepare to be immersed in a world where order is not essential, discovery knows no bounds, and the joy of reading comes alive in extraordinary ways.

-

# Prologue

## PREVIOUSLY IN *KING OF THE STREETS...*

The door to the large storage locker was pulled up, and a dim light was on in the corner. Nicolás Muñoz entered the locker and closed the door behind him. He was dressed in a tan Kiton suit, white dress shirt, and Mezlan crocodile shoes. The odor of bloody flesh filled the small area. Nicolás removed his suit jacket and draped it over a chair that in the corner of the room. The odor bounced around Nicolás' nostrils. The scent was intoxicating to him. Nicolás loosened his tie and rolled up the sleeves of his dress shirt. He walked toward the center of the storage locker, toward a naked man that was curled up in the fetal position on the ground. The man was lying in a pool of his blood. Deep lacerations covered his face and body. Four men stood in each corner of the storage locker, each of them in possession of machetes.

"El hijo de puta," Nicolás muttered before spitting on the man. He hovered around, circling the man like a vulture in the sky. "Esto es lo que hacemos a las serpientes," he announced proudly.

Although the sight before him pleased his dark soul, he wasn't happy about the reason behind the man's unforeseen fate. Treachery had reared its ugly head.

Nicolás grabbed a crate from the corner of the storage locker and placed it just above the male's head, before sitting on it. His heartbeat was steady, his palms were dry, and there was no expression on his face. He felt betrayed but didn't show it. The man that he rested his eyes on was once considered an ally, and now it was time to cut all ties with the traitor.

"I guess you didn't think we were going to find out," Nicolás whispered into one of the bloody ears before pulling out a stack of papers that he had rolled up in his back pocket. He threw the papers down at his feet, just in the line of sight of the man's swollen eyes.

"You know what this is? These are the cell phone records from my sons, from the week they went missing. Guess who was the last person they contacted?" There was no response except groans as the pain from the man's wounds began to worsen. "You were texting and calling Alejandro on the same night that I last heard from him. Did you kill my sons, la perra?"

"I di—didn't do this."

SMACK!

"Cállate," Nicolás growled after backhanding the man in the face. "Don't you fuckin' lie to me!" Nicolás closed his eyes for a brief moment. He couldn't help but think about his boys. "Do you know how hard I tried to keep my boys away from this lifestyle? I also tried to keep my daughter away, but they all want to be a part of all of this craziness. My boys didn't find out what I did for a living until they were teenagers. As soon as they found out what I was involved in, they immediately wanted to sell drugs. Do you believe that? They were rich and they aspired to be corner boys. My biggest mistake was raising them in America and not Colombia. They were fascinated with all this Hollywood bullshit. They wanted fame over money, and that is dangerous. They wanted to be known. It is better to move in silence because the more noise you make, the more trouble you invite into your world; trouble like you. I allowed them to be distributors so they would be safe. I thought I could keep them safe. Tell me what you did with my sons."

"I didn't —"

SMACK!

Nicolás backhanded Ramir in the face a second time. The lion's head ring he was wearing left a bloody imprint on Ramir's cheek.

Nicolás reached into his pocket and pulled out a tool. He grabbed Ramir's left hand and positioned his pinky finger between the blades of the pruning shears. Nicolás expected Ramir to begin begging at this point, but the young street soldier was molded to withstand his current situation. Nicolás slowly squeezed the handle of the shears, watching the blades slice into the finger.

"ARRRRGGGHHH!" Ramir screamed at the top of his lungs as Nicolás began to dismember his hand. One by one, Nicolás took away the fingers off both hands. Ramir's screams sent a chill down Nicolás' neck. The young soldier began to fade in and out. He was losing too much blood.

"Uhhh. Th—they weren't who you think they were." Ramir spit out a large glob of blood.

His body ached, and each laceration burned to his core. A stabbing pain in his torso left him balled up on the ground, as a result of several broken ribs. He was so weak and battered; he could barely lift his head to look at Nicolás. The swelling around his eyes blinded him, and the blood that filled his broken nose made it nearly impossible to breathe. This had been the first time Ramir was ever in this type of position. He had always been a hunter, and now he had become the hunted. Even after covering their tracks by disposing of the bodies, cell phones, and vehicles of the Muñoz brothers after killing them, Ramir made one grave mistake. He called them from a traceable number that came back to him, so once Nicolás pulled the phone records, he was able to put the pieces of the puzzle together.

"Where are my sons? Are they alive?"

Ramir coughed up another glob of blood. "I don't know."

"Stop lying. Did your bosses make you do this? Did Cristóbal give you the orders to kill my sons?"

Ramir gathered the last bit of energy he had left. "Fuck you."

Nicolás thought long and hard about anyone who could have been involved in the disappearance of his sons. The Street Kings were the last crew he expected to betray him, especially because the crew was making so much money off his product. There was so much disbelief. Cash even agreed to assist him in the search for his sons. However, since he felt as though The Street Kings had betrayed him, he was ready to send a message. Nicolás grabbed one of the machetes from his henchmen. "Soy el rey de las calles." With one fell swoop, Ramir's head rolled a foot away from his body.

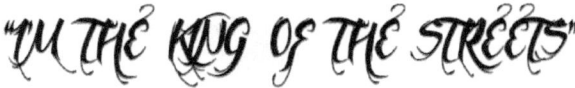

"I'M THE KING OF THE STREETS"

# Chapter 1

Former Detective Ayanna Ali leaned against the cold, graffiti-covered wall of a dilapidated building, her dark curls clinging to her forehead from sweat and rain. Her expressive brown eyes scanned the streets as she clutched her phone tightly in her hand. Life had dealt Ayanna a nasty hand lately – fired from the Atlanta Police Department and dumped by the man she loved, Donovan "Don" King. A whirlwind of emotions raced through her mind: anger, sadness, betrayal, and a longing for something she could no longer have.

"Fuck," she muttered under her breath as she wiped away a tear that threatened to fall. She was a strong-willed woman with a keen sense of intuition, but her heart ached from the void left by Don and being out on these dangerous streets without a badge made her feel more vulnerable than ever.

"Come on, Don," she whispered, dialing his number again. She'd been trying to reach him all day, but he hadn't answered her calls or messages. Ayanna's frustration grew with each unanswered call, her chest tightening with concern.

"Yo, where you at?" she said, leaving another voicemail. "I just wanna talk, a'ight? Hit me back." She ended the call, her thumb hovering over the screen as if contemplating whether to try again. The night air was heavy with tension, and the sounds of sirens and distant gunshots echoed through the streets.

"Okay, okay," she sighed, tucking her phone back into her pocket. "I can do this." Her determination to find Don outweighed her emotional turmoil, and despite the pain, she knew she couldn't let him slip away. Not when there was still so much that they needed to talk about and so many secrets left uncovered.

"Maybe he's at one of his spots," she thought aloud, striding down the street with purpose. As a former detective, Ayanna knew the ins and outs of Atlanta's criminal underworld – and Don, being a member of the notorious Street Kings, had his fair share of hideouts. Ayanna was caught in a precarious position, torn between her duty to her former badge and her love for a drug lord.

"Love don't come easy 'round here," she mused as she navigated the dark alleys and bustling streets. "But I ain't giving up on you, Don. Not yet."

The decision settled in Ayanna's mind like a weight, and she found herself navigating the busy streets of

Atlanta, her eyes locked on Don's luxurious high-rise condo. The towering glass building reflected the vibrant city lights, casting an eerie glow against the darkening sky. The cool night breeze whipped at her dark curls as she approached.

"Damn," she muttered, taking in the grandeur of the building. "Don really knows how to live." Despite her awe, her heart thumped wildly in her chest; fear and determination warring within her.

"Yo, you good?" a doorman asked, giving her a once-over. She nodded curtly, not sparing him a glance before slipping inside. The posh lobby hummed with the chatter of wealthy residents, and Ayanna couldn't help but feel out of place. But she shook off the feeling, focusing on her mission – finding Don.

"Come on, Don," she thought, gripping the elevator railing as it rose to the penthouse floor. "Be here." When the doors slid open, revealing the opulent hallway, she strode forward, her heart pounding louder with each step.

Ayanna hesitated at Don's door, her hand shaking slightly as she raised it to knock. But she stopped herself, opting to use the spare key he'd given her months ago. The lock clicked open, and she stepped inside, bracing herself for what she might find.

"Don!" she called out, her voice echoing through the spacious condo. "You here?" She scanned the pristine living room, her trained eyes searching for any signs of struggle. Nothing seemed out of place, but Ayanna couldn't shake the nagging feeling that something was wrong.

"Where you at, baby?" she whispered, moving through the condo. Her footsteps were hushed against the plush carpet, and she felt like an intruder in Don's sanctuary. The kitchen was spotless. There wasn't a single dish out of place or any indication that Don had been there recently.

"Damn it," she muttered, frustration bubbling up within her. She stepped into the bedroom, her eyes darting over the unmade bed, clothes strewn about. It looked like Don had left in a hurry, but there were no signs of a struggle or forced entry. Ayanna sighed heavily and ran her fingers through her hair.

"Think, girl, think," she urged herself, retracing her steps to the living room. "What am I missing?" She slumped down onto the plush sofa, her thoughts racing as fast as her heartbeat.

Ayanna chewed on her bottom lip, her heart hammering in her chest. Though she found nothing suspicious in Don's condo, she couldn't shake the feeling that something was truly wrong. Her emotions, a whirlwind of worry and fear, clouded her judgment. She tried to focus, to piece together the puzzle, but the uncertainty gnawed at her.

"Shit," she muttered, her fingers tapping nervously on her thigh. In a spur-of-the-moment decision, she grabbed her phone and dialed Sergeant Packard's number. After discovering that he was connected to Cash and Don, she knew he would be able to help. He was tough as nails, but he had a soft spot for her, or so she thought.

"Packard here," came his gruff voice, tinged with fatigue.

"Hey, Sarge, it's Ayanna Ali," she said, trying to sound casual but failing miserably. "I need your help."

"Ayanna? What's going on?" Packard asked, concern etching itself into his tone.

"Look, I know I ain't a cop no more, but something ain't right," Ayanna blurted out. "Don's missing, and I can't find him. I have been calling, and texting—nothing. He ain't here at his condo, either."

"Slow down, girl," Packard said, his voice steady, a calming force amidst the chaos of her thoughts. "You sure he ain't just out enjoying himself, taking a break from all the drama?"

"Trust me, Sarge, I know Don," Ayanna replied, her voice shaky. "He wouldn't just vanish like this. Not without telling me or leaving some kind of clue."

"Alright," Packard sighed. "Let me see if I can cut outta work early and head over there. Send me the address. But you gotta promise me one thing, Ayanna. You stay outta trouble until I get there. The last thing I need is you getting caught up in something dangerous."

"I promise," Ayanna said, her voice barely a whisper. "Just...just hurry up and get here, please."

"I'll see what I can do," Packard replied. "I'll be in touch."

As the line went dead, Ayanna's heart constricted in her chest. She knew the stakes were high and time was running out for Don. But she'd made her promise to Sergeant Packard, and she had to trust that he'd come through for her.

"Come on, baby, where are you?" she murmured as she stared out the condo's window, the Atlanta skyline a shimmering backdrop to her worries.

The sound of a knock at the door jolted Ayanna out of her thoughts. She had been in the condo for hours now, hoping Don would return. She rushed to the entrance, her heart pounding in her chest as she unlocked the door. Sergeant Packard stood there, his tall frame filling the doorway and exuding an air of authority.

"Come on in," Ayanna said, stepping aside to let him enter. Sergeant Packard nodded and brushed past her into the lavish living room of Don's condo. His eyes scanned the space with precision, taking in every detail – from the expensive art on the walls to the sleek leather furniture.

"Nice place," he commented, his voice tinged with an underlying judgment. "Don sure knows how to live it up."

"Can we focus on finding him?" Ayanna snapped, her nerves frayed. Sergeant Packard raised his hands in surrender, his expression softening as he noticed her distress.

"Alright, alright," he conceded. "You said you looked around already?"

"Yeah," Ayanna replied, crossing her arms over her chest. "I didn't find anything that suggests foul play. But I know Don. He wouldn't just disappear like this."

Sergeant Packard sighed and rubbed the back of his neck before walking further into the condo, examining every corner and surface for any clues. Ayanna watched him, biting her lip as her mind raced with worry.

"Look, Ayanna," Sergeant Packard began, glancing at her over his shoulder. "Maybe he just needed some space. You two were going through a rough patch, right? He might've taken off for a bit to clear his head."

"Clear his head?" Ayanna scoffed, her brown eyes flashing with anger. "He could've told me that, Sarge. We have been through a lot together. This –' she gestured around the room, her voice breaking – "this ain't like him."

"Things change. People change," Sergeant Packard said gently. "You've been through a lot too. Maybe he couldn't handle the pressure of everything that's happened, since finding out that you were a cop. And maybe he didn't want to burden you with his own problems."

# AINT NO KING OF THE STREETS

Ayanna's eyes filled with tears at Sergeant Packard's words. As much as she hated to admit it, there was a possibility that Don had walked away from her – from them – without a word. But the thought of living in a world without him made her ache, and she refused to give up on finding him no matter what.

"Sarge, I ain't stopping 'til I find him. I know he's out there somewhere, in trouble, and needing help. I feel it in my gut," Ayanna insisted, her voice thick with emotion.

"Alright," Sergeant Packard sighed, seeing the determination in her eyes. "I'll keep looking into it. But you gotta promise me, Ayanna – don't go chasing after him on your own. You ain't a cop anymore, and this could get dangerous real quick."

"I promise," she whispered, wiping away her tears. "Please help me find him."

Just then, Ayanna's eyes lit up. "Sarge, I also need a favor." she hesitated, eyeing the Sergeant with a mix of desperation and hope. "Can you get a ping on Don's phone? Please, it might be our only lead."

Sergeant Packard frowned, clearly conflicted. On one hand, he knew what it was like to worry about someone you cared for. On the other, he was well aware of the potential consequences of bending the rules, especially when it came to someone connected to the Street Kings.

"Alright, Ayanna," he finally conceded, his voice weary but determined. "I'll see what I can do. But this is off the books – don't go talking 'bout it to anyone, you hear?"

"Thank you," Ayanna breathed, relief washing over her face. She knew she could count on Sergeant Packard.

"Keep in mind, though, it's gonna take a few days to get the results," Sergeant Packard warned, his eyes narrowed in concern. "Don't go doing nothing reckless in the meantime."

Ayanna nodded, swallowing hard as the weight of the situation settled upon her shoulders. "I got you."

With that, Sergeant Packard left the condo, leaving Ayanna to contemplate her next move. The emptiness of the luxurious space weighed heavily on her, a stark reminder of Don's absence. In an attempt to distract herself from her growing anxiety, she busied herself by tidying up the living room and wiping down the kitchen counter. However, her thoughts kept circling back to Don and the possibility that he could be in danger.

As the evening wore on, Ayanna found herself pacing the length of the condo, her fingers drumming nervously against her thighs. She couldn't shake the feeling that something was seriously wrong, and just sitting there waiting for answers was eating away at her.

"Damn it, Don. Where the hell are you?" she muttered under her breath, frustration boiling up inside her. She knew she couldn't just sit around and do nothing – but what else could she do?

Ayanna sat on the plush leather couch in Don's condo, her eyes fixed on the door. She couldn't help but pray that he would walk through it any moment, a smile lighting up his face as he wrapped her in his arms. The silence was suffocating, broken only by the soft ticking of the designer clock on the wall. Ayanna clenched her fists, nails biting into her palms as she forced herself to breathe steadily.

"Come on, Don," she whispered, her voice cracking with desperation. "Just come home."

The hours crawled by, each one more agonizing than the last. Her thoughts spiraled into darker territories, the scenarios playing out in her mind growing increasingly grim. What if Don had been kidnapped? Tortured? Killed?

"Shit," she cursed softly, shaking her head to try and dispel the gruesome images. She needed to stay strong for both of them – whatever might be happening, breaking down wouldn't help anyone.

As midnight approached, exhaustion tugged at the edges of Ayanna's consciousness, but she refused to sleep. She couldn't bear the thought of closing her eyes, only to wake up and find that Don still hadn't returned.

Instead, she paced back and forth across the living room, her steps echoing off the polished marble floors.

"Think, Ayanna. Think," she muttered, her brow furrowed in concentration. "If I were Don, where would I be? Who would I be with?"

She tried to picture Don's friends and associates, but they were all criminals, each one more dangerous than the last. The realization chilled her to the bone – what if Don had finally crossed a line that he couldn't come back from? What if his own people killed him because he was dating a cop?

"God damn it," she growled, pounding her fist against the wall in frustration. "I'm the reason he s missing."

Her heart ached as she remembered happier times when they had been just a regular couple, blissfully unaware of the darkness lurking beneath the surface. But those days were long gone, replaced by secrets and lies that threatened to tear them apart.

"Where are you, Don?" Ayanna whispered, her voice trembling with fear and longing.

As morning light began to seep through the windows, it became painfully clear that Don wasn't coming home. Ayanna sank onto the couch, her body heavy with exhaustion and despair.

"Please be okay," she murmured, tears streaming down her cheeks. "I don't know what I'd do without you."

Her mind raced with possibilities – should she go out and search for him herself? Or wait for Sergeant Packard to deliver on his promise to track Don's phone?

"I need to do something," she muttered, wiping away her tears. She couldn't just sit around and let whatever was happening to Don continue. No matter how dangerous the road ahead might be, she had no choice but to follow it.

"Stay strong, baby," she whispered, her resolve hardening as she prepared to face the unknown. "I'm coming for you."

# Chapter 2

The Atlanta sun blazed down on Ayanna as she walked down the street, her dark curls sticking to her forehead. She scanned the neighborhood, her expressive brown eyes searching for any sign of Don. Everything seemed normal - kids playing in yards, neighbors chatting on porches, and the distant hum of traffic. But something felt off to her, a nagging feeling she couldn't shake.

"Yo, you seen this man around here?" she asked an old man sitting on his stoop, sipping from a brown-bagged bottle. She showed him a picture of Don on her phone.

"Ohhhh, Big Money. Nah, ain't seen him around in a while," he replied, squinting up at her. "You a cop or something?"

"Ex-cop," Ayanna corrected, clenching her jaw. "Just lookin' for my friend."

"Right," he muttered, taking another swig from his bottle. "Good luck with that. If you find him, tell him

# AIN'T NO KING OF THE STREETS

Mr. Doug needs to hold a couple dollars. Young blood always hooks me up when he's around."

Continuing her search, Ayanna's mind raced with possibilities. What if Don had gotten into trouble with the Street Kings? Or worse, the D-Block crew? Images of her past with Don flashed through her head - their late-night talks, shared laughter, and stolen kisses. The memory of her love for him fueled her determination to find him. He was more than just a member of a notorious criminal organization; he was someone who cared about her and who she cared about in return.

"Enough walking," she thought, gritting her teeth. "Time to get serious." Pulling out her phone, she requested an Uber to take her to the Street Kings Club - the last place they were together. If he wasn't there, maybe someone around there would know where he'd gone.

In a matter of minutes, a red sedan pulled up next to her, the driver giving her a nod through the open window. "Ayanna?"

"Yep, that's me," she confirmed, sliding into the back seat.

"This address is a club, right?" the driver asked, checking his phone. "You sure you wanna go there in the daytime? I don't think it's open right now."

"Absolutely," she replied, her voice firm and resolute. She stared out the window as they drove, watching the streets of Atlanta blur past her.

"Guess you know what you're doing," the driver said with a shrug. Ayanna didn't bother responding; her mind was already focused on the task at hand. The club loomed in her thoughts - an ominous presence that held answers she desperately needed.

"Please let Don be there," she silently prayed, her heart pounding in her chest.

The ride to the club was quiet. The driver had the radio on, but it was low. As they rode through the streets of Atlanta, Ayanna looked at every vehicle. She hoped to see a familiar face driving by, but it was a failed effort. As her head remained on a swivel, the Uber driver finally pulled up to her destination. Ayanna exited the vehicle and just stared at the building.

As Ayanna approached the club, she noticed the front door bolted shut with a heavy padlock. Her heart sank, but she knew better than to give up so easily. She circled around the building, searching for another way in.

"Damn," she muttered under her breath, scanning the graffiti-covered walls for an opening.

Her eyes landed on a half-open back door, hidden away in a dark alley. A sense of conflict washed over her; she wasn't a cop anymore, and breaking into private property could land her in serious trouble. But she couldn't shake the feeling that Don needed her help.

"Ah, screw it," Ayanna decided, gripping the cold metal handle and pushing the door open. It creaked loudly, echoing through the empty alleyway. Before she entered, she hesitated, pulling out her phone. She dialed Sergeant Packard's number, hoping he'd answer and provide some guidance.

"Come on, Sarge," she whispered urgently as the call rang unanswered. Finally, the voicemail beeped, prompting her to leave a message.

"Yo, Sarge, it's Ayanna. I'm at the Street Kings Club, and something ain't right. The front door is locked up tight, but the back door's wide open. I dunno if I should go in or not, but I got this feeling in my gut that Don might be in there. Hit me back, man. I need your advice," she said, her voice wavering with concern.

Hanging up, Ayanna stared at the screen of her phone, waiting for it to ring. Seconds turned into minutes, and her patience rapidly dwindled. With a sigh, she pocketed her phone, preparing herself for whatever lay beyond that door.

"Alright, Don," she whispered to herself, taking a deep breath. "I'm coming for you, no matter what it takes."

Bracing herself, Ayanna stepped into the dimly lit club, the stale smell of sweat and liquor hanging heavy in the air. Her heart pounded in her chest as she scanned the room, every shadow seemingly hiding a potential threat. The silence was unnerving, and she couldn't shake the feeling of being watched.

"Hello? Don?" she called out, her voice echoing through the deserted space. She strained to hear any response but was met with only the low hum of the club's electrical system.

As Ayanna ventured further into the club, memories from that fateful night flooded her mind. She could almost hear the thumping bass and laughter of the Street Kings mingling with Don's smooth, infectious chuckle. They'd been celebrating another birthday, the alcohol flowing freely, their bodies swaying together on the dance floor.

*"Damn, girl, you know how to move," Don had teased her, his hand resting possessively on the small of her back.*

*Ayanna smirked, remembering how she'd leaned in close, whispering provocatively in his ear, "You ain't seen nothin' yet, baby."*

*But that playful exchange had turned deadly in an instant when the D-Block crew had stormed in, guns blazing. Instinct took over, and Ayanna had pulled her own weapon, firing a shot that found its mark in one of the assailants. In the chaos that followed, she'd been forced to reveal her true identity as an undercover cop, shattering the trust she'd built with Don and the Street Kings.*

"Focus, Ayanna," she muttered, shaking away the past. This wasn't the time for reminiscing. Don was in trouble, and she needed to find him.

With each step she took, the knots in her stomach tightened. The dark, empty club seemed like a labyrinth filled with treacherous twists and turns. Ayanna knew she was on her own, but that wouldn't stop her from searching for Don. The love they'd shared and the danger he could be in drove her forward; her determination a steady flame burning within her.

"Where are you, Don?" she whispered, her voice cracking with desperation. "I won't give up on you. I promise."

Ayanna crept down the dimly lit hallway, her eyes scanning for any signs of Don or clues to his disappearance. The familiar office door loomed ahead, its once polished surface now marred by scratches and smeared with grime. She hesitated for a moment before pushing it open, her heart pounding like a drum against her ribcage.

"You can do this," Ayanna muttered under her breath as she surveyed the chaos inside the office. Papers were strewn about the floor, and file cabinets gaped open, their contents spilled out like entrails. A shattered picture frame lay in one corner, the remnants of a happy memory now scattered in glittering shards.

"Who did this?" she wondered aloud, her voice barely audible above the distant hum of traffic outside.

Bending down, she sifted through the mess, her fingers brushing against crumpled receipts and torn documents. The evidence of a desperate search was clear, but what were they looking for?

"Something ain't right," Ayanna murmured, her gut churning with unease. As a former detective, she'd been trained to trust her instincts, and every fiber of her being was screaming that danger lurked nearby. But she couldn't afford to back down now; Don's life might be hanging in the balance.

Bracing herself, she stepped back into the hallway and made her way toward the dance floor, her pulse quickening with each step. The shadows seemed to close in around her, whispering sinister secrets that sent shivers down her spine.

"Get it together, girl," she scolded herself, fighting to keep her composure. "You've faced worse than this."

As she entered the dance floor, her eyes struggled to adjust to the darkness. It was here that she and Don had danced, laughed, and shared sensual kisses - but those memories seemed like a lifetime ago now.

"Come on, Don," she whispered fiercely, willing him to appear before her. "Where you at?"

But instead of the man she loved, Ayanna's eyes fell upon a dark, glistening puddle on the floor. Her heart skipped a beat, and she instinctively recoiled, the coppery scent of blood assaulting her senses.

"Shit," she hissed, her voice trembling with fear. She knew that this gruesome discovery meant that time was running out for Don - if it hadn't already. But she refused to let panic cloud her judgment; she needed to think clearly and gather as much information as possible.

"Who are you beefing wit', Don?" she questioned softly, racking her brain for any enemies he might have made along the way. Suddenly, she remembered the D-Block crew and the night she'd been forced to take the life of one of their leaders. Could they be responsible for this?

"Damn! Why didn't I see this coming?" Ayanna berated herself, her frustration mounting. Her gaze remained locked on the ominous puddle of blood. Her instincts kicked in and she scanned the room for any other clues or signs that might point her in the right direction.

"Oh my God!" she gasped as her eyes drifted upward to the balcony above her. There, hanging from the railing like a grotesque marionette, was a bloody corpse. The head had been severed from the body, making it impossible to tell if it was Don or someone else.

"Aw, hell naw..." Ayanna's heart thudded painfully in her chest, her breathing shallow and rapid. Tears poured from her eyes and her knees felt as if they were about to give out. Unfortunately, she found what she was looking for. This wasn't just a simple beatdown or revenge - this was something darker, more sinister. She could feel the cold fingers of fear creeping up her spine, threatening to paralyze her with terror.

Ayanna knew she couldn't stay - the situation was far too dangerous for her to handle alone. But her conscience gnawed at her with every step she took toward the exit. If that was Don up there, she owed it to him to find out the truth and bring his killer to justice.

"Don," she said softly, her voice barely audible over the pounding of her own heartbeat. "If that's you... I'm gonna find out who did this. I promise."

With one last glance at the grisly scene, Ayanna shoved open the back door and slipped into the daylight, the chill air outside doing little to quell the storm of emotions raging within her. As she sprinted down the alleyway, she couldn't shake the feeling that danger was lurking around every corner, waiting to pounce as soon as she let her guard down.

But no matter how scared she was, she refused to give up. She'd come this far, and she wasn't about to back down now. Don meant everything to her, and she'd do whatever it took to uncover the truth - even if it meant risking her own life in the process.

"God help me," she breathed, disappearing into the darkness of the night.

# AIN'T NO KING OF THE STREETS

The alleyway swallowed Ayanna whole, her heart pounding in her chest like a jackhammer. The cool air burned her lungs as she tried to catch her breath, the weight of what she'd just seen pressing down on her. Her hands shook with adrenaline as she fumbled for her phone, desperately needing to hear another human voice.

"Pick up, damn it," she muttered under her breath, the ringing in her ear heightening her anxiety. When Sergeant Packard's voicemail kicked in again, she cursed, frustration and anger bubbling up inside her. "Sarge, you need to get your ass over to Street Kings Club now. There's blood, and... and a body hanging from the balcony. I don't know if it's Don, but we gotta find out."

She ended the call, her voice trembling, and forced herself to continue walking down the street, her legs feeling like they might give out beneath her at any moment. The familiar sights of the neighborhood did nothing to ease her unease; if anything, they only served as a stark reminder of how much things had changed since she'd first gone undercover.

"Shit, Don," she whispered, her eyes filling with tears as the possibility that he was gone forever began to sink in. "What the hell happened to you?"

As Ayanna continued down the street, she couldn't help but feel an overwhelming sense of dread creeping up her spine. Though she was no longer a cop, her instincts told her that something wasn't right - that she was being watched, followed even. She glanced over her shoulder every few steps, her paranoia growing with each passing moment.

"Get your head straight, girl," she told herself, forcing back her fear and focusing on the task at hand.

Her determination renewed, Ayanna pressed on, each step bringing her closer to the truth - and, she feared, to the heart of darkness itself. The city seemed to close in around her, its gritty streets hiding a thousand secrets just waiting to be uncovered.

"Bring it on," she muttered, steeling herself for whatever lay ahead. "I've come too far to back down now."

And with that, Ayanna disappeared into the streets of Atlanta's criminal underworld, guided only by her unwavering resolve and the hope that justice would prevail in the end.

# Chapter 3

The motion lights on the exterior of the club cast an eerie glow on the back alley, flickering over the graffiti-covered walls and trash-littered pavement. The air was thick with the stench of rotting garbage, urine, and stale alcohol as the smell of blood and flesh from inside the club crept out through the back door. It was early in the evening when police responded to an anonymous call about a body that was discovered dangling from a balcony inside the club.

Atlanta Police cruisers arrived on the scene, their sirens piercing the evening silence. The officers emerged from their vehicles, dressed in standard dark-colored uniforms with shiny badges gleaming under the streetlights. They carried an assortment of equipment on their belts: handguns, batons, flashlights, handcuffs, and radios. As they approached the crime scene, the beam of their flashlights illuminated the gruesome sight of the mutilated corpse.

"What the hell," muttered Officer Jenkins as he surveyed the area. "What kind of sick bastard does this?"

"Stay focused, Jenkins," replied Sergeant Packard, his voice stern and unwavering. "We've got to secure the scene and find out what happened here."

The officers on the outside moved with precision, setting up a perimeter with yellow crime scene tape and preventing any onlookers from getting too close. As they worked, the tension in the air grew heavier, each officer acutely aware that they were dealing with something far more sinister than they'd initially suspected.

"Any sign of the club's owner?" asked Officer Martinez, glancing around nervously.

"Nothing yet," responded Packard, his brow furrowed in concentration. "But we're not leaving until we find him or any leads to his whereabouts."

As the officers continued their investigation, the gravity of the situation weighed heavily on them. With the mutilated corpse serving as a grim reminder that the streets of Atlanta were far from safe, they knew they had to work quickly and efficiently to bring justice to the deceased.

"Martinez, get the evidence markers and start documenting this mess," Sergeant Packard barked, his eyes scanning the club's dim interior.

"Copy that, Sarge," Officer Martinez replied, pulling the numbered plastic markers from his kit and gingerly stepping around the bloodstained floor.

"Jenkins, find any witnesses and bring them to me. We need to know what went down here," Packard continued, his voice low and steady.

"Got it, boss," Jenkins said, his face pale as he headed towards the small crowd of civilians that was starting to form near the entrance.

As the officers worked the scene, Packard pulled out his cell phone and dialed Ayanna's number. He knew she had to have some answers that might give some insight into the brutal scene. As the phone rang, he glanced up at the lifeless body, his gut churning with unease.

"Hey, Sarge," Ayanna answered on the second ring, her voice subdued but alert.

"I got your messages. We found the body at the club - it ain't pretty," he said, cutting straight to the point. "Listen, we need your help. Do you know who this is?"

There was a brief silence on the line before Ayanna spoke again. "I... I don't know, Sarge. I got outta there as soon as I could and the body was too far up for me to get a look at it. If I were to guess, I would say it's Don. He's still missing. Did you find anything at the scene? Any leads?"

"Nothing concrete yet but stay by your phone. We might need you on this one," Sergeant Packard told her, his voice strained with the weight of the situation. He ended the call and slid the phone back into his pocket, his mind racing through the possible connections to the body.

"Boss, I found someone who saw something," Jenkins called out, guiding a trembling woman towards Sergeant Packard. "Her name is Wanda."

"Alright, Miss," Sergeant Packard said, shifting into professional mode. "I need you to tell me everything you saw and heard over the last week."

As Wanda recounted the week's events, her voice shaking with fear, Sergeant Packard listened intently, searching for any clues that could lead them closer to unraveling the mystery surrounding the body.

*****

Ayanna paced back and forth in Don's living room, her heart pounding in her chest. She clenched her fists tightly as she tried to calm herself. Sergeant Packard had called her about the dead body, but the fear that gripped her now was not knowing if the body was Don. The last time they'd spoken, there had been tension between them, and Ayanna couldn't shake the feeling that something was wrong.

"Damn it, Don," she whispered under her breath, rubbing her temples. "Why is this happening to you?"

Her phone buzzed in her pocket, startling her. It was Sergeant Packard again. She hesitated for a moment before answering.

"Sarge, did you find something?" Ayanna asked, her voice wavering slightly with concern.

"Listen, we traced Don's phone to New Jersey," he said, his tone urgent. "The tech boys picked up a signal from one of those cell tower triangulation things. You know how it works."

"New Jersey? What the hell is his phone doing there?" Ayanna's breath caught in her throat, her mind racing with possible scenarios.

"Can't say for sure, but I need you to check it out. Can you handle this?" Sergeant Packard asked, knowing full well that sending Ayanna might blur the lines between duty and personal feelings.

"I'm on my way out there now," she replied, determination hardening her voice.

She grabbed her jacket and Don's car keys, heading out the door. As she drove, her thoughts were conflicted - worry for Don mixed with anger at him for involving himself in something so dangerous. Ayanna knew she had to stay focused, but her emotions were threatening to overwhelm her.

The drive from Atlanta to New Jersey was long and arduous. Ayanna fought fatigue and anxiety, stopping only for gas and the occasional cup of coffee. Finally, she reached the location where Don's phone had been traced to. The area was dark and desolate, a stark contrast to the busy city streets she was used to.

She scanned the area for any signs of him or his phone. She parked the car and decided to continue on foot, cautiously making her way through the dimly lit streets.

As Ayanna searched, she encountered obstacles in her path - broken glass, discarded trash, and even a couple of menacing-looking stray dogs that bared their teeth at her. But she pressed on, driven by the need to find Don and ensure he was safe.

"Please, let him be okay," she whispered to herself as she continued her search, fighting back tears of frustration and fear.

*****

Back at the club, a haunting scene unfolded. The lifeless body of an unknown male hung grotesquely from a rusty hook, his mutilated corpse swaying gently in the dimly lit nightclub. Officers worked diligently to secure the area, using tools and techniques ingrained in them through years of experience.

"Alright, let's get it down," Sergeant Packard ordered, signaling for two officers to approach the gruesome display. They donned their gloves and carefully removed the body from its macabre suspension, laying it out on the cold, hard floor.

"Jesus, look at him..." one officer muttered, surveying the carnage. The head and limbs had been severed with brutal precision, his once-strong build reduced to a mangled mess. The team examined the wounds closely, noting every sickening detail as they documented the grisly scene.

"Where the hell is his head? Where are the hands and feet?" another officer asked, barely containing his revulsion.

"Whoever did this must've taken them," replied a third officer, shaking her head in disbelief.

It was then that Detective Jeffrey Knowles, clad in his signature detective outfit, emerged from the back door. His piercing brown eyes locked onto the corpse, recognition dawning on him like a chilling sunrise. He strode towards the body, concern etched into the lines of his face.

"Damn... that's Ramir," Knowles muttered, swallowing the lump that had formed in his throat. "That's Ramir Newton." He'd known Ramir back when he was still alive, a member of the notorious Street Kings. The two had shared a mutual respect, despite being on opposite sides of the law.

"How the hell do you know that?" an officer asked.

Detective Knowles slid a glove on his right hand, before bending over and removing an object that had been placed into the sliced neck. "The Jack of Hearts,"

Knowles said, removing the bloody playing card. "Ramir is – I mean was the Jack of Hearts."

"Knowles, what are you doing here?" Sergeant Packard questioned, eyeing him suspiciously.

"Got word there was a body at the club and figured I'd come take a look," Knowles answered, not taking his eyes off Ramir's remains. "Never thought I'd see him like this, though."

"Neither did we," Sergeant Packard replied coldly. "But this is a homicide scene, Knowles, and you ain't part of this unit. You need to leave."

"Man, fuck that," Knowles shot back, his anger flaring. "I knew who Ramir was, and whoever did this to him probably just started a war. I'm not going anywhere until I find out what happened."

"Look, I know you have some bad blood between you and the Street Kings," Packard conceded, "but you can't let your emotions cloud your judgment. We've got a job to do here, and you're not a part of it. Now go on, get out of here."

Detective Knowles clenched his fists, barely containing the fury that threatened to overwhelm him. He couldn't just walk away from this - not when someone he knew was lying there, butchered like an animal.

"Fine," he finally spat, turning on his heel and storming out of the warehouse. "But you better believe

I'll be watching every move y'all make on this case. And if you slip up, I'll be right there to pick up the pieces."

As he left the crime scene behind, Detective Knowles' thoughts turned to Ayanna, who was out there searching for Don. He needed to make sure she was okay, and that she knew about Ramir's death. But as he pulled out his phone and dialed her number, there was no answer. A chilling dread crept into his gut, gnawing at him like a ravenous beast.

"Pick up, Ayanna. Please, damn it, pick up..."

There was no answer. The line rang and rang, the empty sound of each unanswered call only heightening his dread.

"Shit," he breathed, hanging up after the third attempt. He knew he should keep trying, but the thought of Ayanna being lost or hurt somewhere was too much to bear. Instead, he slammed his fist against the steering wheel, cursing himself for not being there for her.

"Think, Jeff," he told himself, trying to push back the panic that threatened to consume him. "You've gotta find Ayanna before it's too late."

As Detective Knowles started the engine and peeled onto the Atlanta streets, his resolve hardened. He wouldn't let Sergeant Packard or anyone else stand in his way: not when Ayanna's life might be hanging in the balance. He was going to get answers, no matter what it took.

The air hung heavy with tension as Detective Knowles sped through the dark, rain-slicked streets of Atlanta, the city lights reflecting off his car's windshield in a dizzying blur. His thoughts raced like the engine's hum, a mix of anger and worry fueling him as he gripped the steering wheel tightly.

"Shit's not right," he muttered, weaving through traffic with determination. His phone buzzed on the passenger seat, another missed call taunting him.

"Damn, girl," he whispered, urgently tapping redial and holding the phone to his ear. "Pick up the damn phone."

"Jeff, man, you gotta chill," he told himself, trying to steady his breathing as the line continued to ring. Images of Ramir's mutilated body and the unknown fate of Ayanna flashed through his mind, intensifying his unease. He knew he couldn't afford to lose focus: not now when so much was at stake.

"Yo, what the fuck?" A sudden horn blared, snapping him out of his thoughts. He swerved to avoid a collision, cursing under his breath as his heart hammered in his chest. He needed to keep his head in the game.

"Think, man," he repeated, his voice strained. "You gotta find Ayanna and figure out what happened to her. You're the only one who can put these pieces together."

As he navigated the labyrinth of streets, his instincts screamed at him, urging him to press onward.

But just as he began to feel a flicker of hope, his phone rang once more.

"Please be Ayanna," he prayed, snatching it up without checking the caller ID. But instead of her voice, he was met with the gruff tones of Sergeant Packard.

"Knowles, you better have a damn good reason for being out there," Sergeant Packard growled, his words dripping with venom. "I told you to stay the hell away from this case."

"Look, man," Knowles replied, barely masking his frustration. "Ayanna's in trouble, and I need to find her. Don't worry about me—just focus on Ramir's murder."

"Your personal issues are not my concern," Sergeant Packard snapped back. "I want you off the streets and back in your precinct, or so help me, I'll make sure you'll never work in this city again."

"Fine," Knowles spat, his anger boiling over. "Do what you gotta do, but I ain't backing down until I find Ayanna."

The line went dead, leaving Knowles with nothing but the sound of his own ragged breathing. His jaw clenched as he tossed the phone onto the passenger seat, his eyes scanning the shadowy alleys and dimly lit corners for any sign of his friend.

"Where the hell are you?" he whispered, his voice barely audible over the pounding rain. And then, just as he rounded another corner, his headlights illuminated a figure up ahead.

"Jesus Christ," he breathed, slamming on the brakes as his heart leapt into his throat.

The figure stumbled in the darkness, their movements urgent and frantic. But was it Ayanna, or someone else entirely? As Knowles stared through the windshield, unsure of what he was seeing, the streetlights flickered ominously, casting eerie shadows around the figure.

"Please be okay," he whispered, his hand reaching for the door handle. But as he stepped out into the pouring rain, the figure vanished, swallowed by the night.

"Fuck!" Knowles roared, his desperation mounting. Once again, he was left with nothing but questions and an overwhelming sense of dread.

# Chapter 4

The first light of dawn cast long shadows across Detective Jeffrey Knowles' bedroom as he stirred, his dreams tangled with the relentless pursuit of Ayanna Ali and The Street Kings. Rubbing the sleep from his piercing brown eyes, Knowles dreaded having to get up. He reached for his phone on the nightstand, praying for any missed calls or messages from Ayanna.

"Come on, partner," he whispered to himself, scrolling through his notifications. "Give me something."

But there was nothing; her silence only fueled his obsession and deepened his concern. He couldn't shake the reality that Ayanna was caught in the crossfire between her duty and her love for Don. And it tore him up inside, seeing her so conflicted—especially knowing that he would do anything to protect her.

"Enough sitting around," Knowles muttered, swinging his legs over the side of the bed and pushing himself up. He had to see her, had to make sure she was safe. Pulling on his clothes and grabbing his keys, he felt a burning jealousy towards Don, like hot coals smoldering in his chest.

As Knowles navigated the early-morning Atlanta streets, his thoughts raced. What if Ayanna was in danger? What if The Street Kings had gotten to her? He clenched the steering wheel tighter, his knuckles turning pale.

"Focus, man," he told himself, trying to quiet his inner turmoil. "Can't let emotions cloud your judgment."

But it wasn't just about bringing down The Street Kings anymore; it was about saving Ayanna from herself and the dangerous game she was playing. So when he pulled up to her apartment building, the weight of it all pressed down on him like a ton of bricks.

"Please, God," he murmured under his breath, getting out of his car and heading towards the entrance. "Let her be okay."

As he climbed the stairs to her floor, his heart pounded in his ears like a ticking bomb. He dreaded what he might find behind Ayanna's door—but he couldn't ignore the gnawing feeling in his gut any longer.

"Here goes nothin'," he said, steeling himself for whatever lay ahead. With one final, deep breath, Detective Knowles reached out and knocked on Ayanna's door.

No answer came from Ayanna's door, but a cold silence that sent shivers down Detective Knowles' spine. He knew he couldn't stand there waiting all day, so he decided to gather as much information as possible from those who lived around her.

"Got no time to waste," he muttered, his brow furrowed with worry and determination.

He knocked on the first neighbor's door - an elderly woman with a kind face, her hair pulled back into a tight bun. She squinted at him through the peephole, then cracked the door open cautiously.

"Morning, ma'am. I'm Detective Knowles with the Atlanta Police Department. I'm following up on an investigation we have going on. Have you seen Ayanna Ali recently?" he asked, trying to keep his voice steady. He had her picture pulled up on his phone.

The woman thought for a moment before shaking her head. "Nah, can't say I have. But I mostly keep to myself."

"Thank you, ma'am. Please let me know if you see or hear anything," Knowles said, moving on to the next door.

"Will do, Detective," she replied, shutting the door softly behind her.

Knowles continued down the hallway, growing more desperate with each door he knocked on. Most of the neighbors were just as clueless as the elderly woman—unaware of Ayanna's comings and goings or simply too afraid to talk. That was, until he reached the last apartment.

As the door swung open, a burly man with a worn-out baseball cap greeted him. "Detective? Whatcha need?"

"I'm working an investigation and looking for my partner." He held up his phone, displaying her picture. Have you seen anything suspicious lately?" Knowles asked, the urgency in his voice clear.

"Uh, yeah, I did see somethin' weird a couple days ago." The man glanced nervously down the hall before continuing. "There were these Italian dudes knockin' on her door, real persistent-like. Somethin' wasn't right 'bout them, man."

"Did they say anything to you?" Knowles inquired, his heart racing at the mention of potential suspects.

"Man, I ain't gettin' involved. They looked like bad news, ya'know? I just stayed outta their way," the neighbor replied, shifting his weight uncomfortably.

"Understood. But if you see or hear from her, please call me immediately. Here's my card," Knowles said, handing the man his business card and taking note of the neighbor's fear. He couldn't blame him; life around these parts was tough, and everyone had their own battles to fight.

"Sure thing, Detective," the man nodded, pocketing the card as he closed the door.

# AIN'T NO KING OF THE STREETS

Knowles leaned against the hallway wall for a moment, letting the new information sink in. The Street Kings had connections everywhere, but Knowles wasn't aware of any connection with Italian mobsters. If these "Italian dudes" were indeed involved, Ayanna could be in more danger than he'd feared.

"Dammit, Ayanna, what the fuck have you gotten yourself into?" he thought, clenching his fists tightly.

With this lead in hand, he knew there was no time to waste. He needed to find her before it was too late—and he wouldn't let anyone, or anything, stand in his way. His thumbs slammed away his phone screen, as he sent an urgent text message to one of his colleagues.

Knowles marched back down the hallway, his shoes echoing on the worn linoleum floor. He reached Ayanna's apartment door and stared at it for a moment, a pang of concern surging through him. It didn't matter how many doors he'd kicked in during his career; this one felt different.

"Hey! Maintenance!" he barked, a sense of urgency driving his voice. A tired-looking man with a mop and bucket emerged from a nearby closet, raising an eyebrow at the detective.

"Whatchu want?" the maintenance guy grumbled, not impressed by Knowles' authoritative tone.

"Need you to open this door. Police business," Knowles replied, flashing his badge quickly. The man sighed, fumbling with a large keyring before inserting the right key into the lock. The door creaked open, revealing Ayanna's darkened apartment.

"Thanks," Knowles muttered, stepping inside and scanning the room. The maintenance worker lingered for a second before shrugging and disappearing back into his closet.

"Damn it, Ayanna, where are you?" Knowles thought as he flicked on the light switch, illuminating her living space. He took a deep breath, focusing on the task at hand. If Ayanna was in trouble with The Street Kings, he needed to find any traces they might've left behind.

He moved quickly, checking the kitchen counter for any signs of struggle—scratches, broken glass, anything that would give him a clue. But all he found was a half-empty cup of cold coffee and a few scattered papers. *Nothing useful.*

"Focus, Jeff, focus," he told himself, moving on to the living room. His eyes scanned the bookshelves, searching for any misplaced titles or hidden compartments. Every detail mattered; every potential lead could be the difference between life and death.

"Shit, I should have brought some backup," he mumbled, the weight of his responsibility growing heavier by the second.

"Detective Knowles," a voice crackled over his radio, making him jump. He snatched it from his belt, growling into the microphone.

"Knowles here. What is it?"

"I got no intel on those Italian guys you texted me about," the voice replied. Knowles felt his heart rate spike as he listened to the details.

"Keep digging. I'm checking out Ayanna's apartment now. I'll let you know if I find anything."

"Copy that," the voice confirmed before going silent.

Knowles turned his attention back to the apartment, his determination renewed. He had to find something—anything—that would lead him to Ayanna and those responsible for her disappearance. The Street Kings wouldn't get away with this, not on his watch.

"Come on, girl," he whispered under his breath, as though willing Ayanna to give him a sign. "Show me what I'm missing."

"Where else can I look?" Knowles muttered to himself, his eyes scanning the dimly lit bedroom. Knowles began checking her dresser, carefully opening each one and investigating the contents inside.

Knowles' heart started racing as he stumbled upon items that piqued his interest. He slowly ran his hand through Ayanna's underwear drawer, intrigued as the soft under garments brushed across his skin. He grabbed a pair of lace panties, pulling them up to his face and rubbing them across his cheek. He imagined seeing her wearing them, lighting a fire inside of himself.

He shook his head, realizing his focus was slipping and lust was clouding his judgement. He put back the garments and closed the drawer. Knowles turned and continued scanning the bedroom. His gaze fell on Ayanna's laptop, sitting next to her neatly made bed. The screen was dark and silent, like the rest of the apartment.

"Maybe there's something here," he whispered to himself, folding his tall frame into an awkward crouch beside the bed. He flipped open the laptop, fingers tapping impatiently against the keys as it flickered to life. The wallpaper was a photo of Ayanna smiling, her eyes sparkling with happiness. It was a side of her that he hadn't seen in a long time, and it twisted something deep inside him.

"Come on, come on," he urged the computer, his heart pounding in his chest. The laptop seemed to take an eternity to load, the spinning wheel mocking his urgency. Finally, the desktop appeared, cluttered with folders and files. Knowles scanned them quickly, looking for anything that might be related to her disappearance or her involvement with the Street Kings.

"Photos...maybe," he mused, clicking on a folder labeled "Memories." The images that appeared were a mix of personal and professional shots - Ayanna in uniform, laughing with colleagues; candid moments with friends and family. Knowles felt a pang of guilt as he invaded her privacy, but he couldn't afford to leave any stone unturned.

"Hello, what's this?" he murmured, clicking on an album labeled "Jeff & Ayanna." His face softened as the photos loaded, each one a snapshot of happier times. There they were, grinning at each other over steaming cups of coffee, their faces flushed from an impromptu snowball fight. Another photo showed them huddled under an umbrella, rain pouring down around them as they laughed. He remembered that night vividly – they'd been chasing a lead, only to end up soaked and shivering, sharing a moment of warmth amid the chaos.

"Damn, girl," he whispered, his eyes misting over as memories flooded back. He paused on a photo of them sitting on the hood of his car, their hands clasped together, her head resting on his shoulder. "We were good together, weren't we? We were always meant to be more than just friends."

But as he swiped through the photo folders, his smile faded. Images of Ayanna with Don began to appear – stolen moments caught on camera, betraying the depth of their relationship. Knowles clenched his jaw, jealousy and anger boiling beneath the surface.

"Focus, man," he growled, shaking his head to dispel the torrent of emotions. He couldn't let his feelings for Ayanna cloud his judgment now. She was in danger, and it was up to him to find her.

"Jeff, you gotta stay strong," he told himself, taking a deep breath. "Find the clues, save Ayanna, then deal with the rest later."

With renewed determination, Detective Knowles continued sifting through the laptop's contents, searching for any scrap of information that would bring him closer to finding Ayanna and taking down the Street Kings once and for all.

The screen flickered, illuminating Detective Knowles' face as he continued scanning through the images on Ayanna's laptop. He felt a bitter taste in his mouth when he came across more photos of her and Don, their bodies entwined, her hand resting on his chest.

"Fuck," he muttered under his breath, unable to contain his anger any longer. Knowles slammed the laptop shut, the force cracking the screen. "Ayanna, what you doing with somebody like him?"

He paced around the room, his mind racing with thoughts of Ayanna and Don, their secret relationship gnawing at him. The sound of his own breathing echoed in his ears, drowning out everything else.

"Think, Jeff. Think!" He tapped his forehead, trying to focus. "She ain't just gone for no reason. The Street Kings have something to do with this."

"The Italian dudes must be part of it," he reasoned, recalling the neighbor's words. He clenched his fists, his knuckles turning white. "They must've taken her... And it all comes back to Don and those damn Street Kings."

"I'm going to find them, I swear," he whispered, his voice laced with determination and fury. "I'm going to get Ayanna back, and I'm going to make those assholes pay."

His resolve hardened; he knew he had to act fast. Ayanna's life hung in the balance, and every minute that passed could be her last. Detective Knowles grabbed his phone and dialed a familiar number.

"Yo, Mike," he said urgently when his contact picked up. "I need you to run something for me. Check the security cams around Ayanna's place, see if we can spot anyone suspicious. And look into connections between Don and these Italian cats. They got to be connected somehow."

"Gotchu, Jeff," came Mike's reply. "I'll get on it right away."

"Thanks, man," Knowles said, ending the call. He exhaled deeply, trying to regain some semblance of control over his emotions.

"Can't let this jealousy get in the way," he muttered to himself. "Ayanna's life is on the line here."

Gathering every ounce of strength he had, Detective Knowles knew what he had to do: focus on finding

Ayanna and taking down the Street Kings. His determination burned like a fire within him, driving him forward with a single-minded purpose.

"I'm going to bring you home," he vowed, his eyes glinting with steely resolve. "And I'm going to make sure those who are responsible pay for what they've done."

Detective Knowles paced the apartment, his mind racing as he tried to piece together the puzzle. The broken laptop was on the floor, a testament to his anger and frustration. He couldn't shake the nagging feeling that the Street Kings were involved in Ayanna's disappearance.

He grabbed his jacket and stormed out of the apartment, the door slamming shut behind him. He'd search every corner of the city, scour every alley, and interrogate anyone who might have information. He wouldn't rest until he found Ayanna and brought her captors to justice.

As he slid behind the wheel of his car, Detective Knowles felt a fierce determination rise within him. He wasn't just doing this for Ayanna - he was doing it for justice, for the people of Atlanta, and for himself.

"The Street Kings are going down," he growled, slamming his hand on the steering wheel. "And if the Italians are mixed up in this mess, they're going down too."

# AIN'T NO KING OF THE STREETS

With that, Detective Knowles threw his car into gear and sped off into the night, his sights set on uncovering the truth and bringing those responsible to justice. No matter what it took, he wouldn't give up until he found Ayanna and made her captors pay.

# Chapter 5

Detective Jeffrey Knowles rubbed his tired eyes as he stared at the dimly lit computer screen before him. The police station was quiet, save for the low hum of the air conditioning and the distant muffled voices of his fellow officers. The stack of papers on his cluttered desk cast eerie shadows in the dull fluorescent lighting.

"Damn it," he muttered under his breath, riffling through the information Mike had given him about the local Italian organization in Atlanta. Nothing seemed to connect them to the Street Kings or any ongoing investigations. It felt like he was chasing ghosts.

As frustration built within him, Knowles reached for his phone and dialed Ayanna's number. He needed her perspective; she always had a way of seeing things differently. But the call went straight to voicemail, her usual cheerful greeting feeling like a slap in the face.

"Where are you, Ayanna?" he whispered, his voice heavy with concern. He redialed her number, tapping his foot impatiently as the call again went unanswered.

"Knowles, man, you need to chill," Officer Jenkins said, glancing over from his own workstation. "If she ain't answering, she probably busy."

"Mind your business, Jenkins," Knowles shot back, his frustration boiling over. This wasn't like Ayanna; she would never ignore his calls without reason. A gnawing worry began to eat away at him, intensifying his agitation. He dialed her number once more, only to be met with the same outcome.

"Yo, Jeff, you ain't gonna get nowhere blowing up her phone like that," another officer chimed in, shaking his head. "Maybe she just needs some space."

"Y'all don't know her like I do," Knowles responded defensively, clenching his fist around his phone. "Something ain't right." He could feel the weight of their judgment, but he couldn't shake the sense of foreboding that consumed him. He needed to find Ayanna and make sure she was safe.

"Man, we're just looking out for you," Jenkins said, raising his hands in surrender. "We don't want you losing your edge over a woman."

"Edge?" Knowles scoffed, slamming his phone down on the desk. "This ain't about no edge, man. This is about loyalty. Y'all wouldn't understand."

"Whatever you say, detective," Jenkins replied, rolling his eyes and returning to his work.

Knowles took a deep breath, attempting to regain his composure. He knew he couldn't let his worry for Ayanna derail his focus on the case. But as the unanswered calls continued to haunt him, he couldn't help but feel the walls closing in around him.

Frustrated, Knowles decided to redirect his focus on the Ramir homicide case. He pulled up the files, searching for any information that could lead him closer to the Street Kings. His eyes skimmed over the documents until he found what he was looking for - the club where Ramir's body had been strung up.

"Shit," he muttered under his breath as he realized that the club was registered to Cash and Don. The realization fueled his growing hatred towards the gang, and he could feel the anger boiling inside him.

"These motherfuckers got their hands in everything," he growled, clenching his fist and slamming it down on the desk. The sound echoed throughout the room, drawing the attention of other detectives.

"Yo, Jeff, you good?" one of his coworkers asked, raising an eyebrow at the outburst.

"Hell no, I ain't good. Did y'all know that the Street Kings own that club that the body was found in?"

The other detectives looked at each other, wondering where Knowles' random obsession with the Street Kings came from.

"Man, you need to let that shit go," one of them said, shaking his head. "We're all working on different cases here."

"Let it go? Let it go?" Knowles spat out, his voice rising. "You don't understand. Those assholes are responsible for countless deaths in this city. And who knows who else they will kill in the future?"

The other detectives exchanged uneasy glances, unsure of how to handle Knowles' sudden outburst.

"Look, Jeff, we all want to see justice served," another detective said, attempting to calm him down. "But we have to be smart about this. We can't just go on a vendetta against a gang without solid evidence. Besides, we aren't in the homicide unit."

Knowles knew they had a point, but he couldn't shake the anger that continued to consume him. He felt helpless, like justice would never be served for Naomi or any of the other victims of the Street Kings.

As he sat there stewing in his frustration, his eyes focused on the crime scene photos of Ramir's body. His heart hurt at the thought of someone stringing his old partner up in the same manner, like a hog in a butcher's shop.

"Have any of y'all heard from Ayanna today?" Knowles inquired, trying to suppress his rage.

"Nah, man," another detective replied with a shrug. "Haven't seen her around."

"Maybe she's just caught up in some shit," another chimed in, smirking as he continued, "Or maybe she's working with them Street Kings. You never know what the retirement plan for dirty cops is these days."

Knowles felt a surge of offense at the suggestion, his jaw tightening as he shot back, "Ayanna ain't like that. She's one of us."

"Relax, man," the first coworker said, trying to diffuse the tension. "We're just messing around."

"Y'all better watch your mouths," Knowles warned, his voice low and dangerous. "Ayanna's been through hell and back. She don't need this kind of shit."

"Okay, dude. Don't blow a gasket," the second detective conceded, raising his hands in the air. "We'll lay off on the jokes about your corrupt ex-partner."

Knowles slammed his fist down on the table, making his colleagues jump. "You think this is a joke?" he growled, glaring at each of them in turn.

"Jeff, we didn't mean it like that," one detective stammered out.

"Then how the hell did you mean it?" Knowles retorted, his frustration and anger bubbling to the surface. "Ayanna has put her life on the line for this department, and y'all wanna talk shit behind her back?"

"Easy, man," another said, shifting uncomfortably in his seat. "We're just blowing off steam, alright? We all know Ayanna's solid."

"Damn right she's solid," Knowles snapped. "And if I hear any more of this crap, someone's gonna get my boot up their ass."

"Calm down. We get it," the first detective said, raising his hands defensively. "No more jokes about Ayanna. Promise."

"Good," Knowles grumbled, turning away from them as he continued to pore over the case file, his mind racing with thoughts of Ayanna's safety and the growing threat of the Street Kings.

At that moment, the door to the unit swung open, revealing their supervisor, Sergeant Harris. His stern expression immediately cut through the tension in the room. "What's going on in here?" he demanded, eyeing Knowles and the other detectives.

"Nothing, sir," Knowles replied quickly, swallowing his anger.

"Doesn't look like nothing," Sergeant Harris countered, stepping further into the room. "I don't need my detectives and officers at each other's throats. We got enough problems on our hands without all this animosity."

"Apologies, Sarge," one of the other detectives murmured.

"See that it doesn't happen again," Harris warned before turning his attention to Knowles. "Detective Knowles, a word?"

"Of course, sir," Knowles responded, following Sergeant Harris out into the hallway. As they stepped away from the others, he couldn't help but feel a mixture of relief and dread at what his superior might have to say.

"Listen, we just got word of a fire over in Bankhead. It's bad, real bad. I want you and a few other detectives to head over there and start investigating," Sergeant Harris instructed, his voice low and urgent. "I don't need to tell you that Bankhead is a hellhole, so watch each other's backs."

"Understood, sir," Knowles replied, his jaw clenched with determination. He already suspected that the Street Kings might have something to do with this latest disaster. They were a cancer in Atlanta, and their criminal activities were seemingly never-ending.

"Good," Sergeant Harris said, giving Knowles a firm pat on the shoulder. "Get your gear and round up Detectives Jackson, Garcia, Myers, and Rodriguez. You're all going together."

"Will do," Knowles nodded, heading back into the unit to gather the others. As he approached them, he couldn't help but express his frustration. "Damn Street Kings," he muttered under his breath. "They think they can just burn down our city without consequence?"

"Easy, Knowles," Detective Jackson cautioned, sensing the anger bubbling beneath the surface. She was a tough-as-nails detective who had proven herself time and again in the field. "We don't know for sure it's them yet."

"Let's be honest, though," Rodriguez chimed in, his voice tinged with exhaustion. "It probably is. Those bastards have their hands in everything around here." The young detective had been on the force for only a few years, but he'd seen more than enough to understand the scope of the Street Kings' influence.

"Either way, let's get moving," Myers urged, adjusting his worn-out baseball cap. The veteran detective had been around long enough to know that standing around talking wouldn't get results.

"Right," Knowles agreed, grabbing his bulletproof vest and firearm from his locker. "Time to get some answers."

As Knowles and the other detectives geared up and headed out, he couldn't shake the feeling that every step forward brought him closer to uncovering the truth about the Street Kings and their connection to Ayanna. But he also knew that the deeper he delved into this darkness, the more dangerous it would become for everyone involved. And with each passing moment, his determination only grew stronger.

# Chapter 6

The night air was thick with smoke as Detective Knowles and his team arrived at the scene, the charred remains of a row home smoldering before them. Knowles stepped out of the unmarked police car, his piercing eyes immediately scanning the smoldering remains of the house. The acrid scent of burnt wood and melted plastic assaulted his nostrils as he took in the scene. Flames still licked hungrily at the charred skeleton of the building, while firefighters fought to contain the blaze.

"Damn," said Detective Rodriguez, as he exited his vehicle and stood beside Knowles. "This must've been one hell of a blaze."

"Street Kings," Knowles muttered under his breath. His obsession with taking down the notorious gang had consumed him lately. He couldn't help but see their handiwork in every violent crime he investigated.

"Let's find out what happened here," Rodriguez said, striding past the yellow crime scene tape.

"Detectives," a uniformed officer called out as he approached. The young man looked pale and shaken, clearly rattled by the devastation before them. "We got forty-three shell casings on the street. Looks like there was a shootout, but we haven't found any suspects yet."

"Forty-three?" Knowles repeated, his brow furrowing in concern. "Any witnesses?"

"None that we've found so far, sir," the officer replied, his voice cracking slightly. "Neighbors heard the gunfire and an explosion, but nobody saw anything."

"Keep looking," Knowles ordered, his voice cold and authoritative. "I want every inch of this street searched for evidence. And I want those casings bagged and tagged ASAP."

"Yessir," the officer said, saluting before hurrying off to relay the orders.

Knowles turned to Garcia, his jaw set in determination. "We need to find out who did this, and fast. If the Street Kings are behind it, they won't hesitate to strike again."

"Agreed," Garcia said, nodding solemnly. "But we're gonna need more than just shell casings to pin this on them."

"Then let's get to work," Knowles said, his eyes narrowing as he surveyed the chaotic scene before him. His mind was already racing with possibilities, trying to piece together the puzzle that lay in the ashes and debris.

As the detectives and officers combed through the wreckage, it became increasingly apparent that this was no ordinary act of gang violence. The sheer scale of the destruction, the number of lives affected – it all pointed to something bigger, something far more sinister. And if Detective Jeffrey Knowles had anything to say about it, the Street Kings' reign of terror would soon come to an end.

As Detective Knowles strained his eyes, scanning the charred remains of the once beautiful house, a young officer approached him, clutching a clipboard. The acrid smell of burnt wood still hung heavy in the air, sticking to his throat like tar.

"Detective Knowles," the officer said, his voice shaking slightly as he tried to maintain composure. "We just got some intel on the owner of the house. It's registered to Naomi Ikawa."

"Shit." The word slipped out of Knowles' mouth before he could stop it, his heart clenching at the news. *Deuce's sister.* That made this personal – not just for Deuce, but for Knowles too. He'd had dealings with the kid earlier in the week and knew how fiercely he loved his family. And now this? It was like pouring gasoline on an already raging fire.

"Spread the word," Knowles growled, his brown eyes hardening into flint. "If we find any survivors, we interview them immediately. We owe it to this family."

"Yessir," the officer replied, scribbling down notes before scurrying away.

"I know for a fact Cash, Ace and Don did this," Knowles muttered under his breath, his fists clenching at his sides. He knew they were involved somehow and could feel it in his bones. And he wasn't about to let them get away with it. Not this time.

"Detective!" Another officer jogged up to Knowles, panting for breath. "Just got word from the hospital. They got a shooting victim that came in not long ago. I think it might be related to this case. We have two officers on their way there now."

"Has the victim talked to anyone yet?" Knowles demanded, his mind racing with the potential implications of this new development.

"No, sir, he's still unconscious. But they figured we should know, given the timing and all."

"Get a few more uniforms down there to survey the area and gather evidence. I want to be the first one he talks to when he wakes up," Knowles ordered, already turning on his heel and striding back toward his car. Garcia hurried to catch up.

"Jeff, you sure about this? We still got a lot to do here," Garcia pointed out cautiously, glancing back at the smoldering ruins.

"Trust me, this is important," Knowles replied, his voice tight with conviction. "If this guy's involved, he might have information we need to bring down the Street Kings once and for all."

"Alright, man, if you say so," Garcia agreed reluctantly, knowing better than to argue with Knowles when he was in this state. "Just be careful, alright?"

"Always am," Knowles replied tersely as he climbed into his car and slammed the door. He could feel the urgency of the situation pressing down on him like a heavy weight, and he knew he had no time to waste. As he started the engine and peeled away from the scene, his mind raced with thoughts of Deuce's sister Naomi and her tragic fate at the hands of the ruthless gang.

"Naomi Ikawa," he whispered to himself, committing her name to memory. "I promise you that justice will be served this time."

As he drove toward the hospital, Detective Knowles braced himself for the difficult conversations that lay ahead. If the shooting victim was indeed connected to the case, he would have to tread carefully to extract the necessary information without causing further harm.

Upon arriving at his destination, Detective Knowles burst through the hospital doors, his heart pounding in sync with the urgency of the situation. The sterile smell of antiseptic filled his nostrils as he scanned the bustling emergency room for any sign of the officers who'd been sent to watch over the shooting victim.

"Detective Knowles," a voice called out from the far corner. Two uniformed officers, Levis and Tate, stood by a closed door, their expressions tense.

"Give it to me straight," Knowles demanded as he approached them, his graying hair sticking to his forehead with sweat, his trained eyes locked onto theirs. "What's the patient's condition?"

"Stable, but critical," Officer Levis reported, her voice wavering slightly. "The doctors say he's lucky to be alive."

"Has he said anything?" Knowles asked, his mind racing with the potential implications of this new development in the case.

"Nothing useful," Officer Tate chimed in, his arms crossed over his chest. "He ain't cooperating with us. Keeps refusing to talk."

"Is that so?" Knowles' brow furrowed with frustration. He couldn't afford any delays in his quest for justice. Naomi Ikawa's face flashed through his mind, fueling his determination. "Well, let's see if I can change his tune." He reached for the door handle, hardening himself for the challenges that lay ahead.

"Good luck, Detective," Officer Levis muttered under her breath, her eyes filled with doubt.

"Y'all just keep watch out here," Knowles replied, not bothering to acknowledge their skepticism. He knew he had something to prove, not only to these officers but to himself as well.

As he stepped into the dimly lit hospital room, he was struck by the sight before him. The patient lay motionless on the bed, tubes and wires snaking over his body like an intricate web. The rhythmic beeping of the heart monitor filled the air, a constant reminder of the fragile grip this young man had on life.

"Hey, kid," Knowles began gently, his voice soft but determined. "My name is Detective Knowles. I know you've been through hell, and I don't want to make things any harder for you, but I need your help."

The patient said nothing, his eyes flicking toward the detective with a mix of fear and defiance. Knowles froze when he got a glimpse of the patient's face.

"Deuce," Knowles muttered.

Deuce's eyes locked onto the detective's face and a mix of emotions took over him. "Oh God, not you," he responded, his voice hoarse from disuse.

For a moment, the room seemed to hold its breath, the tension thick and inescapable. Deuce's gaze remained locked on Knowles, searching for some semblance of trustworthiness in the grizzled detective's features.

"I need to know what the fuck happened tonight?" Knowles asked.

"Alright," he whispered, his hoarse voice barely audible. "I'll tell you."

"Good," Knowles replied, nodding firmly. "I'm assuming that Cash and his crew are responsible for this. We're going to take those bastards down together."

Outside the room, the two officers leaned against the wall, exchanging uneasy glances as they discussed Knowles' chances of success.

"Man, ain't no way he gonna get that clown to talk," one officer grumbled, shaking his head. "You heard about his old partner, right? Turned out to be dirty. How are we supposed to trust this guy?"

"Knowles ain't like that," the other officer countered, but doubt laced his words. "He's been putting in good work for years. If anyone can do it, it's him."

"That don't mean shit. I don't put nothing past nobody."

As the officers continued to debate, the door to the hospital room suddenly swung open, and Knowles emerged, his face set in a determined scowl. He strode briskly toward them, his eyes never leaving the floor. The officers waiting outside straightened up as he approached, their expressions a mix of curiosity and skepticism.

"Detective?" Officer Levis called out tentatively as he approached.

"Stay posted on this room," Knowles ordered, not bothering to hide his grin. "That you man in there is Deuce Ikawa. He is now an eyewitness for the Atlanta

Police Department. Make sure nothing happens to him."

As the officers scrambled to follow his command, Knowles allowed himself a moment of satisfaction. He'd secured the first piece of the puzzle, and now it was time to hunt down the rest – no matter how many enemies stood in his way.

Detective Knowles strode through the sterile hospital corridors, his footsteps echoing with determination. His mind raced as he formulated a plan to take down the Street Kings once and for all. Images of Deuce's bruised and battered body only fueled his obsession further – it was time to bring these thugs to justice.

"Damn assholes won't know what hit 'em," he muttered under his breath, clenching his fists at his sides.

As he stepped outside into the night air, the city lights flickered across his face like a siren's call. He knew that somewhere in the shadows, the people responsible for this carnage were lurking, waiting for their next opportunity to strike. But not if he had anything to say about it.

He pulled out his phone and dialed Sergeant Harris' number, barely containing his excitement as the line rang.

"Yes, Detective," came the gruff voice on the other end.

"Sarge, it's Knowles. I got some news you're going to want to hear," he said, his words spilling out in a rush. "Deuce Ikawa was the victim from the fire and has agreed to cooperate – he's identified the Street Kings as the attackers."

"Are you sure?" Sergeant Harris' tone was cautious, but Knowles could sense the underlying interest.

"Damn sure, sir," Knowles affirmed, his chest swelling with pride. "He's ready to help us take them down."

"Good work, Detective," Sergeant Harris replied, a note of approval in his voice. "I'll have to inform the higher-ups. We'll need to move quickly before the suspects catch wind of the witness' cooperation."

"Understood, sir," Knowles replied, his heart pounding with anticipation. "I'm ready to do whatever it takes."

"Be careful, Knowles," Sergeant Harris warned him. "We both know how dangerous these gangs can be. Don't let your personal vendetta cloud your judgment."

"Of course, sir," Knowles assured him, though he couldn't help the surge of anger that ignited within him at the mention of his "personal vendetta." This wasn't just about him – it was about justice for Deuce's sister, and for all the countless lives ruined by the Street Kings.

"Keep me updated on any new developments," Sergeant Harris ordered. "I'll be in touch soon."

"Will do, sir," Knowles replied before ending the call.

As he stood there, the darkness of the night pressing in around him, he couldn't shake the feeling that they were on the cusp of something big. He knew there would be risks, but he also knew that he couldn't back down now. The people of Atlanta deserved better – and he was going to make sure they got it.

"Watch out, Street Kings," he whispered into the night. "Your reign is about to come crashing down."

Knowles took a deep breath, preparing himself for the task ahead. The Street Kings thought they ruled this city and that they could terrorize its people without consequence. But they were about to learn just how wrong they were. And Knowles would be the one to teach them that lesson – no matter what it took.

# AINT NO KING OF THE STREETS

The air in the police station hummed with a charged energy as he hunched over his keyboard, fingers flying across the keys. Knowles' eyes were laser-focused on the screen, each warrant and affidavit that he typed up carrying the gravity of his mission to bring down the Street Kings.

"Yo, Jeff," Detective Ramirez called out from the doorway, a stack of case files under her arm. "I got those ballistics reports you asked for. Seems like our boys are sticking to their usual ammo."

"Good work, Ramirez," Knowles replied, not taking his eyes off the screen. He needed every piece of evidence to make these warrants unbreakable – no loopholes, no chances for the Street Kings to wriggle free once they were in his grasp.

"Also," Ramirez continued, stepping into the office and setting the files on Knowles' already cluttered desk, "Forensics found some prints at the scene. Not much, but it's something. Could help tighten the noose around their necks."

"Excellent," Knowles murmured, a hint of a smile playing at the corner of his mouth. The pieces were starting to fall into place, and with each bit of evidence, he could sense the net closing in around the Street Kings. They would pay for their crimes – for Naomi, for Deuce, and for Ayanna.

"Jeff," Ramirez said, hesitating a moment before continuing, "You sure you're good to keep pushing like this? I mean, we all want these dudes behind bars, but... don't forget to take care of yourself too."

Knowles paused in his typing, glancing over at Ramirez. Her concern was well-intentioned, but he couldn't afford to let up now. The fire within him burned too brightly, fueled by the need for justice.

"Ramirez, I appreciate the concern, but I got to see this through," he said, his gaze determined. "The more time we waste, the more lives are at risk."

"Alright, man, I get it," she replied, before turning to leave. "Just... don't lose yourself in the process, okay?"

Knowles nodded, though he wasn't sure if Ramirez saw it as she exited the room. He couldn't afford to think about himself right now – not when the city he'd sworn to protect was under siege by these criminals.

With renewed determination, Knowles resumed typing up the warrants, each word a hammer blow against the Street Kings' reign of terror. As he finished the last document and hit 'print', he allowed himself a small smile. This was only the beginning – but it was a damn good start.

"Sergeant Harris is right," he muttered to himself, watching as the printer spat out the crisp new warrants. "It's a long road ahead... but I'm ready for the fight."

And with that, Detective Jeffrey Knowles, a man driven by the relentless pursuit of justice, prepared to take the first step towards dismantling the empire of the Street Kings – one warrant, and one arrest, at a time.

# Chapter 7

Detective Knowles, his hair slightly disheveled and heavy bags under his eyes, locked onto the papers before him. He leaned over his cluttered desk and tried his best to review each line of the documents. The fluorescent light above flickered sporadically, casting a harsh glow on the printed warrants he was reviewing. A cigarette dangled from his lips, the ash threatening to fall as he whispered the names of the Street Kings under his breath: Ace, Cash, Don, Nate.

His obsession with taking down the notorious gang had consumed him; it was all he could think about. Every fiber of his being yearned for justice, for the streets of Atlanta to be free from their relentless grip.

"Knowles!" Lieutenant Anderson's voice boomed through the precinct, snapping Knowles out of his fixation. He glanced up, noticing the lieutenant standing in the doorway alongside Captain Therian, both wearing stern expressions.

"Captain, Lieutenant," Knowles acknowledged, rising from his seat. "What can I do for you?"

"We need to talk," Captain Therian said, gesturing toward his office. His tone was grave, sending an uneasy feeling coursing through Knowles.

"Sure thing, Cap." Knowles stubbed out his cigarette, leaving it smoldering in the ashtray as he followed the two ranking officers into the office.

The door clicked shut behind them, and Lieutenant Anderson got straight to the point. "Look, Knowles, we know you've been working your ass off on this Street Kings case, but we gotta set some things straight, ya hear?"

"Your evidence needs to be solid against these guys if we're going to proceed with the case," Captain Therian added, his voice firm yet concerned. "They already made a fool of the Feds for that weak ass case they brought up against them and they have a big lawsuit pending in court because of it. We can't risk our department's reputation on flimsy accusations."

"Understood, Cap," Knowles replied, his jaw tightening. He knew the stakes were high, but he also knew the city needed the Street Kings to be held accountable. "I've got everything we need. I wouldn't have brought this to you if I didn't believe in it."

"Jeffrey," Lieutenant Anderson interjected, her voice tinged with authority as she tried to level with him. "We aren't saying you aren't doing your job the right way. We just need you to understand that these warrants have to be tight. There's no room for error."

"Believe me," Knowles said, his eyes locking onto theirs, determination evident in his gaze. "I won't let anything slip through the cracks. These guys are going down."

Captain Therian leaned forward, his fingers laced together as he stared at Knowles with an intensity that made the detective's stomach churn. "Let me be clear. If these warrants don't hold water — if there's even a hint of doubt in the evidence you present, it won't just be the case that's compromised. It'll cost you your job. Do you understand?"

"Y-yeah, Cap," Knowles stammered, feeling the weight of the captain's words like a vice grip on his chest. He had faced dangerous criminals and survived shootouts, but the thought of losing his job, his purpose in life, was enough to make him sweat.

"Good," Captain Therian nodded, seeming satisfied with Knowles' response. "Now get back out there and make sure everything's in order. Trust but verify, as they say."

"Will do," Knowles replied, giving them a curt nod before exiting the office. As he returned to his desk, he couldn't shake the feeling that something was off. If only he could put his finger on it... But for now, he had work to do, and the sooner he tightened up those warrants, the sooner the Street Kings would face justice.

Back at his desk, Knowles spread out the papers before him, scrutinizing every line of text and every piece of evidence he had against the gang. His mind raced, picking apart potential weaknesses and identifying areas where he could strengthen the case. With each adjustment, he felt a renewed sense of determination, fueled by the desire to see justice served.

"Yo, Jeff," Detective Garcia called from across the bullpen, his voice a mix of curiosity and concern. "You good, man? You look like someone just killed your dog or something."

"I'm fine. Just... working," Knowles responded, his eyes never leaving the warrants. He didn't have time for small talk; the stakes were too high. "Just gotta make sure everything's airtight, you know what I mean?"

"Yeah, man. Just don't forget to breathe," Garcia said with a chuckle before returning to his own work.

Knowles took a deep breath and refocused on the task at hand. The captain's warning echoed in his mind, spurring him to comb through every detail with painstaking precision. He needed this case to be sound, unassailable. Only then could he bring justice to the city and ensure that his badge remained firmly on his chest.

As he fortified the case against the Street Kings, Knowles couldn't shake the lingering dread that lurked in the back of his mind. But he pushed it down, choosing instead to focus on the task at hand. There would be time for doubts later; for now, all that mattered was taking down the gang that had held Atlanta in its iron grip for far too long.

Knowles stared at the screen, his heart pounding in his chest. He knew he had to be certain before sending out the email with the finalized warrants. His fingers hovered above the keyboard, then hesitated. What if there was a piece of evidence he'd overlooked? The consequences were too dire to ignore.

Just to be on the safe side, he decided to secure a digital footprint for the suspects. This would place them at the scene of the crime and would be a key piece of evidence for the case.

"Alright, let's see where you assholes are hiding," Knowles muttered under his breath as he initiated a trace on each of the Street Kings' phones. He watched as three blips appeared on the map – Nate's phone disconnected, Ace in Atlanta, Cash in Baltimore, and Don in New Jersey. "What the hell?"

"Is something wrong, Jeffrey?" Detective Myers asked, leaning against his cubicle wall.

"Look at this," Knowles said, gesturing to the map. "Ace is here in Atlanta, but Cash and Don are in different cities. Why would they split up like that?"

"Maybe they're trying to throw us off their trail," Myers suggested with a shrug. "Or maybe they've got business elsewhere."

"Could be, but it doesn't sit right with me," Knowles admitted, rubbing the back of his neck. "I need these warrants to stick, and if two of them ain't even in town, I might as well throw these warrants in the damn trash."

"Jeff, man, don't get so worked up," Myers tried to reassure him. "You've been at this for hours. You know these guys better than anyone. Trust your instincts."

Knowles looked back at the screen, his brow furrowed with doubt. Trust his instincts? They'd served him well in the past, but this case was different. This was personal. And with his job on the line, he couldn't afford any mistakes.

"Myers, I appreciate it, but I'm not takin' any chances," Knowles said with determination. "If my gut's telling me they're up to something, then I need to figure out what it is."

"I understand all of that," Myers replied. "But just like everyone else has been saying, don't let this case eat you alive. We all want them behind bars, but not if it means losing yourself in the process."

"I told yall I won't. I'm good. I just want to get it right," Knowles said, forcing a weak smile. But as he stared at the map and the scattered blips, he couldn't shake the feeling that something big was about to happen. The Street Kings were known for their coordinated operations, so why were their key players suddenly scattered across the country?

"Dammit," he muttered, tapping his fingers on the desk. He needed more evidence; something concrete to hold against them. And with each passing second, the doubt crept in, threatening to consume him.

But he wouldn't let it. Not now. Not when justice was within his grasp. He'd find the missing piece, the connection between the cities, and bring the Street Kings crashing down.

"Whatever you're up to," Knowles whispered, glaring at the screen, "I'm going to find out. And when I do, you're all going down."

Knowles' hand trembled slightly as he picked up the phone, the weight of his decision pressing down on him. He dialed the familiar number, the one that connected him to F.B.I. Agent Dillon Miles. The line rang twice before it was picked up.

"Agent Miles," came the curt response.

"Hey, Agent Miles. It's Detective Jeffrey Knowles, over at APD," he said, trying to keep the nervousness out of his voice. "I need your help with something."

"Knowles?" Agent Miles replied, a tinge of surprise in his voice. "What's going on?"

"Listen, I got this case. The Street Kings. You remember them, right?" Knowles asked, though he knew the answer already. There was no way Agent

Miles could forget the gang that had slipped through their fingers.

"Of course, I remember those bastards," Agent Miles growled. "What about them?"

"Look, I got reason to believe they're planning something big. I mean, real big," Knowles said, leaning in closer to the phone. "But I don't have enough concrete evidence yet. My gut's telling me there's something going on, but my hands are tied without more proof."

There was a pause on the other end of the line. Knowles could hear the faint rustling of paper, the sound of an office alive with activity. Then, Agent Miles spoke again, his voice low and serious.

"Detective, I'm going to be real straight with you," he began, using Knowles' title in a rare display of authority. "You don't want to go down this road. It's dark, dangerous, and it'll cost you more than you can imagine. You saw what happened when me and my unit tried to take them down. We lost everything, and those sons of bitches walked away scot-free. I'll be lucky if I don't lose my house and my entire life savings in that damn lawsuit they filed against The Bureau and everyone involved in the investigation."

"Dammit," Knowles snapped, frustration rising in his voice. "I can't just sit here and let them keep running the city. I have to do something!"

"I understand how you feel," Agent Miles said gently. "But you need to think about the consequences. If you don't have a rock-solid case, they'll have their attorneys tear you apart. You'll lose your job, your reputation, and God knows what else. Are you really willing to risk all that for a hunch?"

The words struck Knowles like a bullet, forcing him to confront the reality he'd been trying to ignore. He clenched his jaw, letting out a slow breath.

"Look, I appreciate your honesty," he said quietly, struggling to keep his emotions in check. "But I can't just turn my back on this. I need to try."

"Alright," Agent Miles sighed. "But just remember, this isn't some game you can just play when you want. It's life or death. And if you aren't careful, you could end up losing a hell of a lot more than just your job."

As the line went dead, Knowles stared at the phone in his hand, the weight of Agent Miles' words settling heavy on his shoulders. But even as the shadows of doubt and fear crept in, he couldn't shake the burning determination that drove him forward.

"Whatever it takes," he whispered to himself. "I'll bring those bastards down."

With his hands shaking slightly, Knowles snatched up the stack of warrants he had prepared earlier. He stared at them for a moment, torn between fear and determination, before finally setting his jaw and striding determinedly toward the warrant division.

"Hey, Richie," he called out as he approached the desk, trying to keep his voice casual. "I need you to process these for me."

"Sure thing, Jeff," Richie replied, scanning the warrants with raised eyebrows. "Damn, you going after the heads of the crew? You sure you ready for this?"

"Never been more sure," Knowles said, though the doubt gnawed at him from within. Still, he pushed it aside, focusing instead on the image of justice being served.

"You got some balls for doing this," Richie said with a shrug, taking the warrants from Knowles. "Your funeral," he joked.

"Thanks for the vote of confidence," Knowles muttered, turning away and heading back to his desk.

As he sat down, the gravity of what he had just done began to sink in. The warrants were out there now; there was no going back. And as the reality of his situation settled upon him, so too did the realization that he had just waded into waters deeper and darker than he ever could have imagined.

"Shit," he whispered under his breath, rubbing his forehead as he tried to quell the rising panic. "What the hell have I gotten myself into?"

Trying to regain his focus, Knowles opened his computer and pulled up the case files on the Street Kings. As he delved deeper into the gang's world, he couldn't help but feel a chill run down his spine. The corruption they had unleashed upon the city was like a cancer, spreading its tendrils through every layer of society, leaving nothing untouched in its wake.

"Damn," he breathed, his eyes widening as he came across yet another victim of the gang's brutality. "This shit runs deep."

"Yo, Jeff," a voice called out from behind him, startling him out of his thoughts. "You look like you seen a ghost or something."

"Mike," Knowles said, looking up to see his fellow detective standing over him, a worried expression on his face. "Nah, just... working on this case. It's getting to me."

"Look," Mike said, pulling up a chair and sitting down beside Knowles. "I know you're all about justice and taking down these scumbags, but you have to be careful. Everybody knows the Street Kings ain't no joke. They got people everywhere, Jeff. You can't trust anyone."

"Tell me something I don't know," Knowles replied, his voice tense and strained. He glanced at the warrants he had just issued, knowing full well that they could very well sign his own death warrant. But it was too late for second thoughts; he had made his decision, and he would see it through to the end.

"Listen, Mike," Knowles continued, looking his friend in the eyes. "I appreciate the warning, but I can't back down now. These cowards need to be stopped, and if it's gonna cost me my life—or my job—to bring them to justice, then so be it."

"Jeff, man," Mike said, shaking his head, his voice heavy with concern. "I just hope you know what you're doing, because once you go down this path, there ain't no turning back."

Knowles nodded, his expression determined as he met Mike's gaze. "I know. And believe me, I'm ready for whatever comes my way."

As Mike left, Knowles took a deep breath, hardening himself for the long, treacherous road ahead. He knew that going after the Street Kings was a dangerous game, but it was a game he was willing to play. For the sake of Atlanta, for the sake of justice, he would stop at nothing to bring down the gang that had held the city in its iron grip for far too long.

Little did he know, however, just how high the stakes were about to become, or the perilous twists and turns that awaited him as he delved deeper into the world of corruption and danger.

*****

The sun dipped below the horizon, casting long shadows as Detective Knowles walked through the dimly lit streets of Atlanta. His piercing brown eyes scanned his surroundings, searching for any signs of the notorious Street Kings. On every corner, it seemed like there were whispers of their influence, but tonight, he was looking for something more concrete.

"Yo, Jeff!" a voice called out from behind him. It was Officer Daniels, one of the few cops he still trusted. "You got something?"

Knowles shook his head, frustrated. "Nah," he replied, his voice strained. "But I know they're out here somewhere. They ain't gonna leave their turf unguarded. I know for a fact that Cash and Don can't be out of town. If I can catch them in their territory, they won't have a defense later in court. It will be the nail in the coffin that I need to confirm that they carried out that attack on my victim."

"Man, this whole thing's got you spooked, huh?" Daniels asked, concern etching his face. "You sure you want to go down this road? I heard that the Captain and Lieutenant ain't playing when it comes to this crew."

"Can't turn back now," Knowles muttered, clenching his jaw. "I made my bed, and I'm gonna lie in it. They need to be stopped, no matter the cost."

Their conversation was cut short as gunshots rang out nearby, shattering the quiet evening air. A sense of dread washed over Knowles, his heart pounding as he drew his weapon and took cover behind a parked car.

"Shit! Stay down!" he barked at Daniels, who followed suit. Adrenaline coursed through Knowles' veins as his mind raced, trying to make sense of the situation.

"Think it's them?" Daniels yelled over the cacophony of gunfire.

"Only one way to find out!" Knowles shouted back, taking a deep breath and preparing himself for whatever lay ahead.

As the gunfire ceased, Knowles sprang into action, sprinting towards the source of the disturbance. Rounding a corner, he found himself face to face with a group of men, their weapons still smoking from the recent shootout. Their cold, emotionless eyes bore into him, and for a moment, Knowles hesitated.

"Police, don't move," Knowles announced.

Oddly, the men didn't seem startled by the detective's presence. A few of them casually began walking away, while others sized up the rogue detective.

"Thought you could catch us slippin', huh?" Big T sneered. "You might as well put that gun away. You ain't got shit on us, pig." The large man was holding a pistol, but handed off his gun to a teen who took off on a bike with the weapon. The other armed men also took off running, as Knowles approached them. Big T raised his hands in the air and smirked. "No gun, no crime."

"Maybe not," Knowles replied, his voice steady as he leveled his gun at the man. "But I will make sure that you no longer exist in this world."

Knowles was now within a few feet of Big T, who seemed to have the detective's undivided attention. The other men spread out, blocking all escape routes.

"Jeff!" Daniels shouted, arriving just in time to see Knowles being surrounded by the gang members. Half of them had their phones out and were live streaming to social media. "What are you doing, man? We have to call for backup!"

"Too late for that," Knowles replied, his mind racing as he tried to figure out a way to escape the situation unscathed. Suddenly, an idea struck him. "Daniels, grab that bag!" he yelled, nodding towards a duffel bag discarded at the feet of one of the gangsters. "Let's see what our little friends are holding."

"Yo, what's this fool tryna pull?" another gang member demanded. "It ain't nothin' in that nag and no one gave you permission to search it."

"Only one way to find out, ain't there?" Knowles shot back, keeping his gaze locked on Big T as Daniels grabbed the bag and ripped it open.

"Shit!" he exclaimed, his eyes widening in shock. "Detective, it's nothing in here but clothes."

"It can't be," Detective Knowles muttered. Officer Daniels walked the bag over to him, showing him the contents. "Fuck."

"Smile, you're 'bout to be famous," Big T teased, holding his phone up to capture video of the encounter. "Y'all see what these dirty ass pigs do to us in our own neighborhoods. He just walked up to us with his gun out and he's illegally searchin' our shit. We need to defund these mothafuckas."

Knowles' heart sank as he realized the gravity of the situation. He had been set up, and there was no way out. The Street Kings had won once again, and he may have just lost everything. He could only imagine what his bosses' reactions would be once the videos of him with his gun pointed at the men went viral.

But he refused to go down without a fight.

"Listen to me, you scum," he growled, his eyes burning with fury. "I may be down, but I'm not out. You can try to silence me, but I won't stop fighting. I'll bring down your entire organization, no matter what it takes. Mark my words."

The gangsters laughed, sneering at him as they backed away. "Yeah, we'll see about that, pig," one of them said, flipping him the bird as they disappeared into the night.

Knowles stood alone, his heart pounding as he contemplated his next move. He knew that he was in deep trouble, but he also knew that he couldn't give up. Not now, not ever.

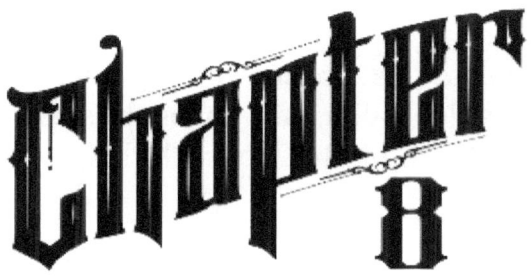

# Chapter 8

Detective Knowles tossed and turned as he struggled to get comfortable. He had been tossing and turning all night, the events of the past week continuously haunting him. The alert from his phone gave him a reason to get up but his head was spinning. Although his mind was telling him that it was time to get an early start to the day, his body wanted to stay put. Fatigue weighed him down, only giving him enough energy to reach over towards his phone at the edge of the bed. Knowles knocked over the empty bottle of tequila as he grabbed his phone and checked the message from Officer Daniels.

**Ofc. Daniels: Yo, Knowles, check this out.**

Knowles clicked on the link that was attached to the message. He pressed play, and his heart dropped like a lead weight in his chest. There, on the screen, was the Street Kings' associate Big T, surrounded by his crew. The shaky footage captured Knowles illegally stopping them and pulling a gun on Big T, his face a mask of rage.

"Look at this crooked cop right here!" shouted Big T in the video, calling him out on the street for everyone to hear. "He thinks he's above the law 'cause he got that badge, huh?"

"Man, fuck this pig!" added one of his crew members, laughter echoing all around.

Knowles could feel the blood draining from his face as he watched the video unfold, his hands gripping the phone so hard his knuckles turned pale. His obsession with taking down the gang had led him to cross a line, and now the evidence was spreading like wildfire.

"Shit," he muttered under his breath, realizing the potential damage this video could cause. If his superiors saw it, he'd be done for. His career, his reputation, everything he'd worked for – gone in an instant.

In a blind panic, Knowles made up his mind: he had to find Big T and get that video taken down, no matter what it took. But as he rushed out of bed, his conscience nagged at him, forcing him to confront the moral dilemma he now faced. Was he willing to compromise everything he stood for just to save his own skin?

"Damn it," he hissed, slamming his fist against the steering wheel. "What the hell am I doing?"

As he sped through the rough streets of Atlanta, his mind raced with the possible consequences of his actions. Would taking down Big T justify breaking the very laws he'd sworn to uphold? Could he reconcile his quest for justice with the dirty tactics he was now employing?

"Focus," he told himself, trying to shake off the doubts that clouded his thoughts. "You've got a job to do."

But deep down, Knowles couldn't escape the creeping feeling that he was about to make a terrible mistake – one that would change his life forever.

As Knowles pulled into a run-down gas station, the grimy neon glow of the overhead lights seemed to be hypnotizing him. It was as if it was a sign from a higher power for him to turn around and go home. Knowles reached for his phone, his fingers shaking as he dialed Officer Daniels' number.

"Yo, Daniels," he said, trying to keep his voice steady. "I need you to do something for me. I need you to find Big T and confiscate his phone."

"Wait, what?" Daniels replied, his voice laced with disbelief. "Man, that's illegal. You know we can't go around taking people's property like that without a warrant."

"Damn it, Daniels!" Knowles snapped, his grip tightening on the steering wheel. "This is serious! If that video stays up, I'm finished!"

"Jeff, listen to yourself," Daniels said, his tone softening. "You're letting your emotions get the best of you. Think about what you're asking me to do. It ain't right, man."

"Fine!" Knowles barked, hanging up in frustration. He slammed his phone down on the dashboard, his mind racing.

Desperate, he began scrolling through social media, searching for any trace of the damning video. To his dismay, he found that several users had already shared it, each one racking up thousands of views. Panic welled up inside him, threatening to suffocate him.

"Shit, this is bad," he whispered, his eyes welling up with tears as he scrolled through the comments, each one more hateful than the last. The realization that his career might already be beyond saving settled heavily on his shoulders.

"Focus," he told himself, wiping away the tears that threatened to blur his vision. "You're a damn good detective. You've faced worse than this."

But as he stared at the screen, the cruel words of the anonymous commenters echoing in his head, Knowles couldn't help but feel that this time, it was different. This time, there might be no way out.

"Damn you, Big T," he growled, slamming his fist against the steering wheel once more. "I'll make you pay for this if it's the last thing I do."

Knowles reached into his glove compartment and grabbed the half-empty bottle that was inside. He opened the tequila bottle and put it to his lips, sucking down the strong liquor. With a newfound sense of determination, Knowles started his engine and pulled back onto the dark streets of Atlanta, the weight of his moral dilemma growing heavier with each passing moment.

Rain pelted the windshield as Knowles' unmarked car rolled through the heart of the Street Kings' territory. The biting wind howled through the cracked window, carrying with it the scent of decay and desperation. He gripped the wheel tightly, his hands tight with tension.

"Shit," he muttered, scanning the shadows for any sign of Big T or his crew. His heart pounded in his chest, threatening to burst free.

A flicker of movement caught his eye, and he eased the car to a stop. Up ahead, beneath a flickering streetlight, Big T stood surrounded by a handful of his goons. They were laughing, completely unaware of Knowles' presence.

"Got you now, you son of a bitch," he whispered, drawing his gun and stepping out into the rain.

"Hey!" he shouted, his voice a mix of fury and fear. "Big T!"

The laughter died abruptly, and the gang members turned to face him. Their eyes were cold and hard, like chips of ice.

"Hey, it's the Dirty Detective?" Big T drawled, an amused smirk playing across his lips. "What brings you back to our humble abode? You trynna make another video?"

"Cut the shit," Knowles spat, leveling his gun at the gang leader. "You think that video's gonna scare me off? You're dead wrong."

"Maybe you ain't heard, man," one of the goons chimed in, a malicious grin spreading across his face. "It's going viral. The whole world knows that you're a fuckin' snake."

"Shut your mouth!" Knowles barked, trying to keep his terror in check. "I want that video taken down, Big T. Right now!"

"Or what?" Big T countered, his voice dripping with disdain. "You'll threaten to shoot me again? We both know how that worked out for you last time."

"Look, I'm not playing," Knowles snapped. He drew his weapon from the holster, his finger twitching on the trigger. "I ain't gonna let you destroy everything I've worked for. You take down that video, or I swear to God..."

"Or what?" Big T repeated, taking a menacing step forward, his crew closing ranks behind him. "You really think you can take us all on, detective? As soon as you pull that trigger, you're a dead man."

As Knowles stood his ground, the tension in the air thickened. From every corner and alleyway, members of Big T's crew emerged, their shadows creeping along the filthy pavement as they surrounded him.

"Seems like you got yourself in a bind, detective," Big T taunted, his cold eyes locked onto Knowles'. "I'll give you one chance to walk away. No harm, no foul."

Knowles hesitated for a moment. Thoughts raced through his mind, each one more dangerous than the last. In the end, though, his obsession with justice won out. With a determined glare, he swung the butt of his gun across Big T's face, sending him sprawling to the ground.

"Take down that video, or I swear to God I'll put a bullet in your brain!" Knowles snarled, aiming his gun at Big T's head. He could feel the adrenaline coursing through his veins, fueling his desperation.

"Yo, chill!" Big T shouted, blood dripping from the corner of his mouth as his crew closed in around Knowles. "You really think you gon' get away with this? You ain't above the law!"

"Shut up!" Knowles yelled, his voice cracking with emotion. He knew he was losing control, but the thought of his career going up in flames fueled his rage even further. "I'm tired of all you lowlifes ruining my city!"

"Fine, detective," Big T spat, wiping the blood from his lips. He gave a nod to his crew, and within seconds, they were on Knowles. Fist after fist rained down on him, driving him to the ground in a chorus of pain and anger.

Knowles fought back, carelessly swinging his weapon and trying to pistol whip any of the attackers. His semi-drunken state made him an easy target as he got hit repeatedly. He holstered his weapon and shielded himself from the blows.

"Stop! Please! You can't do this." Knowles gasped, his arms raised defensively over his face. He could feel the blows weakening him, and in the back of his mind, he knew he was losing this fight.

"Pathetic," Big T sneered, watching as his crew pulled back, leaving Knowles battered and bruised on the pavement. "You ain't no better than us, detective. We both do what we gotta do to survive."

As Knowles lay there, gasping for breath, he couldn't help but question the choices that had led him to this point. Was he just as corrupt as the criminals he pursued? Had his obsession with justice turned him into a monster?

Big T's goons moved in like a pack of lions on an injured gazelle. They had the detective surrounded and a few of them were ready to make the kill. Detective Knowles had a feeling that this would be the end as he braced for the final blows. "Finish his ass," Big T ordered, as his men punched on the detective.

"Freeze!" Daniels' voice cut through the air like a knife, causing the violent scene to come to an abrupt halt. The sound of sirens filled the night as several police cars screeched to a stop, their strobing lights painting the alley in blue and red.

"Shit, it's the cops!" one of Big T's crew members yelled, and they scattered like cockroaches, leaving Knowles lying on the ground, his face bloodied and bruised.

"Jeff, what the hell happened?" Daniels asked, rushing to his side, a look of concern etched across his face.

"Get off me," Knowles snapped, shoving Daniels away as he tried to help him up. "I don't need your damn pity."

"Man, this ain't about pity," Daniels retorted, his eyes narrowing. "You were supposed to be investigating, not looking for a fight. You lost your cool, Jeff. You let them get to you."

"Damn right I did," Knowles spat, wiping the blood from his lip with the back of his hand. "And I'd do it again if it meant taking down those motherfuckers."

"Even if it means breaking the law?" Daniels challenged, his voice laced with disappointment. "You're better than that, or at least I thought you were."

"Enough!" Knowles barked as he pushed himself up, staggering slightly under the weight of his injuries. "We got bigger fish to fry than this little disagreement." He glanced around at the chaos left behind by the Street Kings' escape, his jaw set with determination. "I need to talk to the Captain."

"Jeff, maybe you should think about sitting this one out," Daniels suggested cautiously, but Knowles wasn't having it.

"Back off, Daniels," he growled, his eyes blazing with defiance. "This is my case, and I'll see it through to the end."

With that, Knowles limped away from the scene, leaving Daniels and other officers standing there, torn between his loyalty to their fellow officer and his duty to uphold the law. He headed back, to get ahead of this situation.

Once he got back to the station, Knowles locked himself in the bathroom, wincing as he examined his battered reflection in the mirror. His face was a mess of bruises and cuts, a painful reminder of the line he had crossed in his pursuit of justice.

"Fuck," he muttered under his breath, dabbing at the blood with a wet paper towel. "I gotta get my shit together." He knew he couldn't afford to let his emotions cloud his judgment any further; not when so much was at stake.

Knowles dug in his pocket and removed the travel-size mouthwash, opening it and taking a swig. He allowed the mint fluid to swish around his mouth before spitting it into the sink. A combination of blood, saliva, and mouthwash rinsed down the drain. With a heavy sigh, he finished cleaning up and headed for Captain Therian's office, preparing himself for the confrontation to come.

"Captain," Knowles said, his voice strained as he stood in front of the boss' desk. "I need your help. We gotta find Ayanna – she's the key to all of this. She will have information on the Street Kings that none of us can get. She was the only one on the inside and I'm sure if we find her, she'll be willing to help us take them down."

Therian eyed him warily, taking in the bruised and battered state of Knowles' face. He leaned back in his chair, folding his hands over his chest. "Former Detective Ali is no longer with the force," he replied, his tone measured. "She got her own mess to deal with, and we got ours."

"Captain, you know she's still got connects in the streets," Knowles pressed, feeling a spark of anger rising within him. "We need her intel."

"Knowles, I can't just drag her back into this life when she's already out," Therian argued, his face growing stern. "Besides, how do you expect me to trust someone who's been playing both sides?"

"I'm sure she has a good explanation for what she did."

"And I'm in no mood to entertain anything she would have to say. The decision that was made is well above my pay grade, so there is nothing I can do about it." Therian stared at Knowles, taking in the bruises and cuts that marred his face. "You look like hell, detective," he noted dryly. "Are you sure there isn't something else you need to tell me?"

"Not at all, sir," Knowles replied, his gaze never faltering. At that moment, Knowles realized he had to play his trump card. "Oh, there something I wanted to mention to you." With a resigned sigh, he reached into his jacket pocket, pulling out a stack of papers. "I got the signed arrest warrants back from the judge," he said, slapping them onto the captain's desk. "This is our chance to take them down once and for all."

Therian raised an eyebrow, clearly taken aback by the sudden turn of events. He leafed through the warrants, his expression unreadable. Knowles could feel the tension in the air, thick and suffocating. He knew he was asking for a lot, but he couldn't shake the feeling that Ayanna was the missing piece they needed.

"Fine," Therian relented, his voice low and gravelly. "But you better make damn sure that everything in these warrants stick. I won't have my department compromised any further."

"Understood, Captain," Knowles replied, feeling a sense of purpose surging through his veins. "I'll do whatever it takes to bring these criminals to justice."

"Alright," Therian said, standing up from his desk. "Get ready to move. We're gonna hit the Street Kings where it hurts."

Knowles nodded, already mentally preparing for the battle ahead. He knew the road would be fraught with danger, but he was determined to see it through – for the people of Atlanta, for the police force, and for himself. With a renewed sense of conviction, he turned on his heel and strode out of the captain's office, ready to face whatever challenges he would have to face in the days to come.

The captain's office door slammed shut behind Knowles, the sound echoing in his ears like a starting gun. His heart raced with determination as he headed down the hallway, the fluorescent lights flickering overhead.

"Knowles!" Therian's voice boomed from behind him, stopping him in his tracks. "I almost forgot –" The captain tossed him a set of keys, the metal jingling together as they spun through the air. "You're gonna need backup. Assemble a team you can trust."

"Thanks, Captain," Knowles replied, catching the keys and pocketing them. He knew exactly who he wanted on this mission – cops that would have his back no matter what.

"Remember, we ain't got time to waste. I want the Street Kings off our streets, pronto," Therian warned, his voice heavy with urgency.

"Understood," Knowles said, nodding firmly.

As soon as Therian disappeared into his office, Knowles hit the ground running. He burst into the detective bullpen, the buzz of conversation and clatter of keyboards filling the air. It was time to put his team together.

# Chapter 9

Detective Knowles started his day off with a hot cup of coffee and a ton of optimism. He had a full day ahead of him, putting together an arrest team for the heads of the biggest criminal organization in the city. Despite his video with Big T still circulating the internet, Knowles did his best to put that fiasco in the back of his mind. He planned on coming clean to his bosses after the arrests, hopeful that the big operation would overshadow his poor judgment on that day.

Knowles pulled into the precinct parking lot, driving Captain Therian's unmarked pickup truck. He was grateful that his boss trusted him with the pristine vehicle. It was an upgrade from Knowles' beat-up Chevy Impala. It had been a long night, and he could feel the weight of his responsibilities bearing down on him like the humidity that clung to the air.

"Today's the day," he muttered to himself. "We're gonna take down the Street Kings once and for all."

As he walked through the station, officers and detectives nodded at him with a mix of admiration and skepticism. Some of them were wary of Knowles because of his connection to his former partner, but they couldn't deny his dedication to the case.

"Listen up!" Knowles shouted, commanding the attention of the room. "I've got the green light to bring down the Street Kings, and I need a team ready to roll ASAP! If you are down, let me know."

"Count me in, man." Officer Daniels approached, a rigid glint in his eyes. Despite their recent conflict, Knowles couldn't help but respect the officer's commitment to the cause.

"Good to have you, Daniels," Knowles acknowledged, grateful for the unexpected support.

"Who else?" Knowles scanned the room, searching for familiar faces of those who'd been by his side before. Officer Jenkins, a burly man with a shaved head and an intimidating scowl, nodded in agreement.

"Let's do this, Knowles," Jenkins growled, his voice hoarse from years of smoking. "I'm sick of these punks running our city."

"Thanks, Jenkins. We're gonna take them down for good this time," Knowles said, his resolve only growing stronger.

"I'm in," Ramirez shouted.

"Me too," Myers followed. "I want to put my cuffs on that Cash dude; the one that everybody calls the King of the Streets."

"Ain't No King of the Streets," Knowles roared, pounding his fist on the desk. "The streets belong to us."

More officers and detectives volunteered for the operation, each of them eager to be a part of the biggest case of the year.

"Ya'll got room for one more?" Garcia chimed in, his dark eyes filled with determination.

"Absolutely," Knowles replied, grateful for the fierce loyalty he'd shown him throughout their years working together. "Let's get moving."

With his team assembled, Knowles felt a renewed sense of purpose. He knew they were walking into danger, but there was no turning back now. The Street Kings had haunted Atlanta for far too long, and it was high time they met their match.

As they all filed into a conference room, Daniels caught up to Knowles, his expression serious. "Jeff, are you sure you're ready for this? After what happened with Big T..."

Knowles cut him off, his jaw set. "I've never been more ready, Daniels. It's time we ended this once and for all."

He strode into the conference room and stood in front of the large whiteboard; there was a detailed map of Atlanta sprawled across it. He studied the known Street Kings' hideouts, his brow furrowed in concentration. The room was filled with the low hum of anticipation as his team prepared for what could be their most dangerous mission yet.

"Alright, everyone, listen up," Knowles barked, commanding the attention of the detectives that surrounded him. The weariness in his voice was masked by his determination. The room fell silent, every eye on him. We've got one shot at this, so we need to make it count. We're gonna arrest every last one of them. We currently have arrest warrants for the heads of the organization, but you better believe that there will be more to come. We will split into four teams and execute all four warrants simultaneously. We hit them hard and we hit them fast. No hesitation."

"Got any intel on their total numbers?" Detective Jackson asked, her fingers drumming nervously on the table. As a seasoned investigator, she had seen her fair share of action, but this was different – this was personal.

"Can't say for sure," Knowles admitted, his gaze never leaving the map. "But we aren't going in blind. We'll have eyes on the ground, feeding us updates. We'll be ready for whatever they throw at us."

"Damn straight," Detective Martinez chimed in with confidence.

Knowles glanced around the room, taking in the faces of his team. These were the people he trusted most; the ones he knew would have his back no matter what. They were family.

"Remember, we're doing this for Atlanta," Knowles continued, locking eyes with each detective and officer in turn. "These scumbags have terrorized our city for far too long. It's time we took it back."

"Let's get it," Daniels said, a steely resolve in his eyes. Despite their earlier conflict, he was all in.

"Now, our key eyewitness is Deuce Ikawa. He is the most recent victim of the Street Kings and was shot after they set his sister's home on fire. For those who don't know, Naomi Ikawa is Deuce's sister. Naomi was a cooperating witness for the F.B.I. and went missing, along with her young children, prior to the court hearing. Her brother suspects foul play at the hands of the Street Kings but as of right now, no bodies have ever been discovered. She is still in the system as a missing person. We need to do everything we can to make sure that the same thing doesn't happen to our witness."

Heads nodded around the room; their expressions grim but focused. Knowles knew that they all understood the stakes – if they failed, the streets would only become more dangerous, and Deuce's life would be a sacrifice for the cause.

"Speaking of Deuce," Knowles continued, "There are two officers with him at the hospital. I would like at least four with him at all times. Once he recovers, we can have him moved to a secure location immediately to await court proceedings. But until then, he is our priority. Understood?"

"Got it, Detective," replied Officer Myers, a tall, wiry man with a bushy mustache. "I'll head over to the hospital with my partner. We'll make sure he's safe."

"Good," Knowles nodded, his eyes scanning the room for any sign of doubt or hesitation. He couldn't afford to have anyone on his team wavering in their commitment. "Now let's figure out the teams and develop these plans."

The detectives and officers huddled around the table, poring over the plans they'd devised together. They discussed entry points, escape routes, and possible contingencies, each one trying to predict the Street Kings' actions before they happened. The tension in the room was uneasy, but so was the sense of urgency.

It was not going to be an easy operation, trying to strike all four men at one time. In the back of his mind, Knowles knew that Cash and Don were out of state. He planned to bulk up the teams going after Ace and Nate, knowing that the other two teams would probably see minimal action.

Detective Soto burst into the room and leaned against the table, his muscular arms crossed over his chest. "I just got some intel from an informant. They said that Ramir's funeral is coming up in a couple of days," he said, a somber tone in his voice. "It's supposed to be packed with Street Kings and other local gangs under them."

Detective Knowles eyed him thoughtfully as the gears turned in his head. "That might be our best shot," he finally said, tapping a finger on the table. "We get them when they're all gathered together. They won't know what hit them."

"Damn straight," Lieutenant Anderson chimed in, his eyes narrowing. "We need to map out every damn move we make for this operation. There is no room for mistakes."

The team began to work out the details, tracing routes on maps and marking potential sniper positions. Knowles could feel the pressure mounting, each decision feeling like it carried the weight of the world. He knew there was no turning back now - this was their chance to bring down all of the Street Kings once and for all.

"Hey, Knowles," Captain Therian called, gesturing for him to follow him and Lieutenant Anderson into a corner of the room. The captain's gruff voice echoed through the room as he spoke. "You know how high the stakes are, right? We can't afford to mess this up at all."

"Of course, sir," Knowles replied, his jaw clenching with determination. "I understand the risks, but I believe in this plan."

Lieutenant Anderson placed a hand on Knowles' shoulder, her eyes stern but not unkind. "Jeffrey, we're counting on you. You've been wanting to lead this investigation, and now you have the chance to bring it home. Don't let us down."

"Understood, ma'am," Knowles said, nodding. "I won't fail you, or the department."

"Good. We appreciate everything that you are doing for the department. The higher-ups haven't forgotten that you are the one who tipped off the Internal Affairs Division about Detective Ali and her connection with this gang. If everything goes right with this case, there may be a promotion in your future."

Knowles felt a thrill run through him at the mention of a promotion. It wasn't something he had been actively seeking, but the idea of being recognized for his hard work was certainly appealing. However, he quickly pushed the thought aside, knowing that his focus needed to be solely on the mission at hand.

"I appreciate the consideration," Knowles said, his voice steady. "But right now, my priority is getting these criminals off the streets and bringing justice to the victims."

Captain Therian nodded approvingly. "That's the attitude we like to see, Knowles. Keep that mindset and you'll go far."

As the captain and lieutenant returned to the table, Knowles took a deep breath, his mind racing with thoughts of the upcoming operation. He knew that he couldn't afford to let doubt creep in, not when so much was riding on his shoulders.

"Alright, team," he said, clapping his hands together to refocus the room. "Let's get back to work. We've got a funeral to crash and some Street Kings to put behind bars."

# Chapter 10

Rain streaked down the stained-glass windows of the Atlanta church, casting a somber kaleidoscope of colors across the pews. The air was thick with tension and the scent of damp wool as mourners gathered to pay their respects to Ramir. Despite the solemn atmosphere, an undercurrent of danger pulsed beneath the surface.

Detective Knowles stood near the back, his graying hair slicked down and his bloodshot eyes surveying the room. He adjusted the cuffs of his coat, the fabric chafing against the concealed weapon holstered at his side. Knowles had spent years trying to take down the Street Kings, and now, with the murder of Ramir, he could sense that things were reaching a boiling point. It was only a matter of time before the powder keg of violence exploded.

"Everyone in position?" Knowles murmured into the small radio tucked behind his ear. His undercover team, consisting of seasoned detectives and fresh-faced rookies alike, had arrived early to stake out the funeral. They had taken up strategic positions throughout the church, blending in with the mourners while keeping a watchful eye on the entrances and exits.

"Affirmative," came the hushed replies from his team. Each officer knew their role and understood the importance of maintaining their cover. The Street Kings were unpredictable, and it was crucial to be prepared for anything.

As the rain continued to pour outside, the church began to fill with people. There were family members, dressed in black and wiping away tears; low-level drug dealers who owed their allegiance to Ramir; and others whose faces were known to Knowles from his years working the streets of Atlanta.

"Keep an eye on the side entrance," Knowles instructed quietly, feeling the weight of his obsession with the Street Kings bearing down on him. "We don't know who might try to slip in."

"Copy that, Detective," came the response from one of his officers, her voice steady and determined.

The murmured prayers and hushed conversations filled the church as the funeral service began. Knowles couldn't shake the feeling that something was about to go terribly wrong. The air felt charged, electric, like a storm waiting to break.

"Y'all ready for this?" he whispered into the radio, his eyes never leaving the casket at the front of the church. "Stay sharp."

"Ready as we'll ever be," came the grim response from his team members. They knew what was at stake, and they were prepared to stand with Knowles, no matter the cost.

Knowles continued scanning the crowd, his eyes flicking from person to person as they filed into the church. He recognized some of the mourners – Ramir's cousin with the crown tattoo beneath her right eye, some of his high school friends who had somehow managed to avoid getting caught up in the web of crime that had ensnared so many others.

"Wow," he muttered under his breath as a group of familiar faces entered the church. Low-level dealers, the kind who hustled on corners and sold dime bags out of their cars. They were small-time, but they were still connected to the Street Kings. A piece of the puzzle that he was determined to solve.

"I got a visual on some players from the west side," Knowles said into his radio, his voice low and tense. "Stay sharp."

"Copy, Detective," came Officer Daniels' response.

The church doors creaked open again, and this time Knowles felt a jolt of adrenaline as Big T and his crew swaggered inside, their heavy gold chains glinting beneath the dim light of the church. Big T was a known enforcer for the Street Kings, and his presence at the funeral set off alarm bells in Knowles' mind.

"Big T just walked in," he whispered into his radio, trying to keep his tone steady despite the sudden spike in his heart rate. "I'm gonna stay out of sight."

"Be careful, Detective," Daniels warned, his eyes meeting Knowles' from across the room. They shared a brief nod, a silent acknowledgment of the danger they now faced.

Knowles ducked behind a large pillar, using it as cover as he continued to watch the procession of mourners. He knew he needed to keep his focus on the bigger picture – taking down the Street Kings – but the sight of Big T and his crew filled him with an almost uncontrollable urge to act.

"Stay cool, man," he told himself, taking a deep breath to steady his nerves. "We're here for Ramir, not them."

But as the funeral service continued, and the tension in the room grew thicker with each passing moment, Knowles couldn't help but feel that the walls of the church were closing in on him, trapping him in a deadly game of cat and mouse with some of Atlanta's most dangerous criminals.

"Lord, give me strength," he prayed silently, his hand resting on the butt of his gun.

Knowles' eyes scanned the room, his gaze falling on Ace and Nate as they entered with a posse of men. He could see the anger etched in every line of Ace's face – an unmistakable blend of grief and rage that sent shivers down Knowles' spine.

"A couple of the Street Kings just walked in," he whispered into his radio, his attention locked on the pair.

"Copy that," Daniels replied, his voice tense. "Keep an eye on them."

As Ace approached Ramir's casket, he paused, lifting his head to lock eyes with Knowles for a brief moment. The detective tensed, feeling the weight of Ace's stare like a physical blow. Their silent exchange spoke volumes – Ace was watching him, too. The detective's heart pounded in his chest, but he maintained his composure, giving nothing away.

"Stay vigilant, team," Knowles warned over the radio, never breaking eye contact with Ace. "Things might get ugly real quick."

Suddenly, the church doors opened. Ayanna walked in, her dark curls cascading around her shoulders, and his chest tightened. She was with Don, their fingers intertwined, and Knowles couldn't help but feel a pang of jealousy. He clenched his jaw, struggling to keep his emotions in check.

"Yo, Ayanna's here," Knowles whispered into his radio, his words laced with bitterness.

"Looks like they brought some Italian enforcers with them too," one of the officers added.

Knowles stared at the men that accompanied Ayanna and Don. "The fuckin Italians," he said through a clenched jaw. *They weren't a threat to her. They are working with her.*

"Stay focused, Knowles," Daniels replied, his voice a mixture of concern and authority. "We'll deal with that later. Right now, we need to keep our eyes on the prize."

"Copy that," Knowles muttered, willing himself to focus on the task at hand. But he couldn't tear his eyes away from Ayanna as she took her seat, her expressive brown eyes scanning the room before settling on him for a brief moment. That look – it tore him apart. It felt like a lifetime ago that they'd been partners, had each other's backs on the force, and now this? It was almost too much to bear.

Knowles tried to steady his breathing, his heart aching as the church doors opened again and Cash walked in, flanked by Reana. Knowles' eyes widened as he took in the sight of the powerful leader of the Street Kings, accompanied by a gang of women who looked equally dangerous.

"Damn, Cash just got here and he's not alone," Knowles said into his radio, trying to keep his surprise under control. "It looks like he brought some backup with them."

"Roger that," Garcia responded, his voice betraying his own anxiety. "Everyone, be ready for anything."

*This ain't gonna end well*, Knowles thought to himself, his hand gripping his gun a little tighter beneath his coat. He knew that things were escalating quickly, and there was no telling how far they'd go before the day was done.

"Lord, help us all," he prayed silently, his eyes never leaving Cash as he took his seat in the crowded church.

"Okay, team," Knowles said, taking a deep breath. "Let's get ready to make these arrests. We're gonna hit them hard and fast, as soon as the service ends."

"Roger that," came the chorus of responses over the radio. The tension in the air was intense, each officer preparing themselves for the chaos that was sure to follow. Knowles could feel it in his bones – today would be a day to remember, one way or another.

But then, the organ began to play, and the mournful notes reverberated through the church. The pastor began speaking and giving his condolences to the family. Knowles glanced around the room, looking at the solemn faces of those gathered to say their final goodbyes. For a moment, he hesitated.

"Damn," he cursed under his breath, conflicted. This was a funeral, a time for families to grieve and find closure. But then again, these were the Street Kings – they'd caused enough pain and suffering in Atlanta to last a lifetime.

"Knowles?" Daniels' voice crackled over the radio, questioning.

"Stand down," Knowles finally said, his voice heavy with regret. "We'll wait until they're outside the church before we make our move."

"Copy that, boss," Daniels replied, relief evident in his tone. The officers, all of them tense and ready for action, allowed themselves to relax just a fraction, waiting for the right moment to strike.

As the pastor began his eulogy for Ramir, Knowles couldn't help but steal a glance at Ayanna, her eyes glistening with unshed tears. His heart ached, torn between duty and love, knowing that when the time came to make their move, there would be no turning back.

The air in the church grew thick with worry and grief, each breath a mix of sorrow and anticipation. Knowles' heart raced beneath his suit jacket as he studied the faces around him, trying to stay focused on the task at hand while remaining vigilant for any unexpected threats. The soft sounds of sniffling and whispered prayers filled the room, creating an eerie, uneasy atmosphere.

*This is gonna be a mess,* Knowles thought to himself as he surveyed the scene. He could feel the weight of his concealed service weapon against his hip, a constant reminder of the violence that could erupt at any moment.

"Yo, what the hell?" an officer murmured into his radio, voice low and urgent.

"Talk to me," Knowles replied, gripping his gun beneath his jacket. "What's going on?"

"Detectives, I don't know how to say this but... I think we have a problem. There are a bunch of men approaching the church and I think they're armed."

"Shit," Knowles spat under his breath. The funeral had been tense enough with the Street Kings present, but now someone else was coming to add to the chaos.

"Stay cool, everybody. Don't make a move unless they do," Knowles instructed his team, eyes locked on the entrance.

The previously peaceful sanctuary of the church was shattered as the doors were violently ripped off their hinges, and a hoard of armed men rushed in. Panic instantly spread among the funeral attendees as the cacophony of gunshots filled the air, reverberating off the walls like thunderous drums.

"Yo, it's goin' down!" an officer shouted, and in that instant, all hell broke loose.

The gunshots rang out like thunderclaps, echoing through the sacred space and shattering the mournful silence. Mourners screamed and dove for cover, their grief replaced with raw terror. Detective Knowles drew his weapon, aiming at the entrance. His finger pressed against the trigger, but he paused when he noticed who was leading the attack on the funeral.

"Deuce," Knowles muttered under his breath. *What the fuck is he doing here?*

Knowles couldn't believe what he was seeing. Deuce was his eyewitness and the key component needed to take down one of the most dangerous criminal organizations in the country. And now, here he was, leading an armed assault on a funeral.

"Deuce," Knowles yelled, his eyes locked on the young man. "I don't know what the hell you think you're doing, but you're making a big mistake."

Deuce sneered at him, his eyes cold and calculating. he ducked behind one of the Colombians, avowing Knowles.

Knowles gritted his teeth, his grip tightening on his weapon. He knew that he had to take Deuce down, but he also knew that it wouldn't be easy.

"APD! Drop your weapons!" Knowles bellowed, drawing his gun and firing at the Colombians who continued pouring into the church. His fellow officers followed suit, their carefully planned operation now a chaotic battle for survival.

"Damn, they won't stop! The Street Kings are armed too," Officer Daniels cried out as bullets whizzed past him, finding their mark in several of the Colombians. Bodies crumpled to the floor, staining the church's pristine carpet with blood.

"Keep firing, don't let any of them escape!" Knowles ordered. Each shot he took was fueled by his determination to protect the innocent lives caught in the crossfire. In the midst of the chaos, his eyes briefly met Ayanna's – wide with fear and confusion – and he silently vowed to bring her to safety.

"Knowles, I got one of them!" Detective Jackson shouted, triumphantly taking down a Colombian who'd tried to flank her position. "They're starting to back off!"

"Good! Stay on them!" Knowles urged, exchanging gunfire with Deuce himself. The young man's eyes burned with hatred and vengeance, every shot aimed squarely at the Street Kings who had destroyed his life, uncaring about the collateral damage left in his wake.

*Damn it, Deuce!* Knowles thought, ducking behind a pew as bullets shredded the wood just inches above his head. *This ain't gonna bring your sister back!*

In that fleeting moment, Knowles locked eyes with Deuce. Time seemed to slow as both men recognized the unspoken challenge between them. Without warning, Deuce broke into a sprint, shoving mourners out of his way in his reckless escape. The chaos around them erupted once more, screams of panic punctuating the air.

"Deuce!" Knowles shouted, his voice drowned out by the commotion. The young man was fast, but Knowles couldn't let him get away, not after everything he'd caused. "Damn it!" he muttered under his breath, adrenaline pumping through his veins as he took off after Deuce.

"Knowles, where you going?" Officer Daniels called out, trying to keep stray gunfire from reaching the fleeing detective.

"Getting our witness!" Knowles barked back, weaving through the panicked crowd while keeping his focus on Deuce's retreating form. The fallen bodies slowed him down, but he pushed forward, his determination unwavering.

"Y'all cover Knowles, I'll call for backup!" Rodriguez ordered the other officers, her voice urgent yet authoritative.

"Gotcha!" Jackson replied, laying down suppressive fire as she and the others kept the Colombians at bay.

Outside, the rain continued to pour, making the ground slick and treacherous. Knowles nearly lost his footing but managed to catch himself just in time. He could see Deuce ahead, jumping over a parked car and disappearing behind a corner. "You ain't getting away this easy, boy." Knowles gritted his teeth, pushing his aging body to its limits.

"Think you can catch me, old man?" Deuce taunted, his voice filled with bitter rage. He fired off a few shots in Knowles' direction, forcing the detective to take cover behind a nearby dumpster.

"Damn," Knowles muttered, his heart pounding in his chest. He knew he couldn't let Deuce escape, but he also couldn't risk getting shot.

"Knowles, you still with us?" Daniels' voice crackled over the radio, concern lacing his words.

"Y-yeah, I'm still here," he replied, catching his breath. "Deuce is running towards the parking lot. I need some backup!"

"Roger that, we're on our way!" he responded.

"Where are the snipers?" an officer asked.

"We don't have a clear shot," one of the snipers responded, the pouring rain and panicking attendees making it impossible to get a shot at the attackers. "I repeat, we don't have a clear shot."

Deuce's eyes flashed with a wild ferocity as he yanked open the door of a black coupe, the engine already purring in anticipation. Knowles' breath caught in his chest as he watched the young man slip into the vehicle like a snake slithering into its den.

"Shit!" Knowles cursed under his breath, realizing that Deuce was about to escape his grasp. He sprinted towards the car, ignoring the burn in his legs and the ache in his lungs. The rain continued to pour down, soaking him to the bone and blurring his vision.

"Freeze, Deuce!" Knowles shouted, his voice barely audible over the relentless thunder and gunfire. But Deuce didn't hesitate; instead, he slammed his foot on the accelerator and fired off one last shot at Knowles before tearing out of the parking lot.

The sharp, searing pain that tore through Knowles' back knocked the wind out of him, and he stumbled forward, his vision swimming. "God damn it," he grunted, collapsing onto the cold, wet asphalt as blood began to pool around him.

Everything around him began to blur as he gasped for air, his hand reaching for his wound. A bullet fired from inside the church had ripped through his back, just below the coverage of his Kevlar vest. He knew that he was in trouble, that the bullet had hit something vital. His vision began to fade, and he felt himself slipping away.

"No, no, no," he murmured, trying desperately to hold on. He couldn't die here, not like this. There was still so much he needed to do, so much he needed to accomplish.

But then, a figure loomed over him, and he recognized the face of the young man who was toting a pistol and aimed it at Knowles' face. The man held a mixture of anger and regret, and he hesitated for a moment before speaking.

"This is for Big T," the man whispered, his hand trembling as he tried to hold the gun steady. "Dirty ass cop," he followed, firing multiple shots at Detective Knowles before taking off behind the church.

Knowles felt a strange sense of calm wash over him, and he knew that his time was running out.

"Knowles! Talk to me, man!" Daniels' frantic voice crackled through the radio, his worry undisguised even through the static. "Are you okay?"

"H-help," Knowles gasped, fighting to maintain consciousness as the pain threatened to consume him. "I'm hit."

"Stay with us, Jeff," Daniels urged, her tone laced with desperation. "We're coming for you."

As Knowles lay there with his blood seeping into the rain-soaked ground, he couldn't help but notice the carnage that surrounded him. Bodies strewn across the pavement like discarded ragdolls, the pungent scent of gunpowder and blood choking the air. Officers, members of the Street Kings, and Colombians alike, their faces frozen in expressions of shock and agony.

"Damn," Knowles whispered, his vision fading in and out as he stared at the lifeless form of a young officer he'd mentored. "I'm sorry, kid. I didn't... I couldn't..."

"Officer down!" someone shouted nearby, their voice barely audible above the chaos. Knowles knew he should be doing something – anything – to help stem the tide of destruction, but his body refused to cooperate. His limbs felt like lead, his chest aflame with agony where the bullets had torn through him.

"Jeff, just hang on!" Daniels' voice pleaded from the radio, now sounding impossibly distant. "Stay with us!"

Knowles could feel his strength waning, the darkness creeping in around the edges of his vision. He knew he needed to fight – for justice, for Ayanna, for all the lives that had been lost to the brutality of the streets – but it was getting harder and harder to hold onto the will to live.

"Sorry, Daniels," Knowles murmured, his voice barely audible even to himself as his eyes slipped shut. "I tried."

As the chaos continued to rage around him, Detective Jeffrey Knowles succumbed to the darkness, leaving behind a city still plagued by violence and a legacy fraught with unanswered questions.

The End

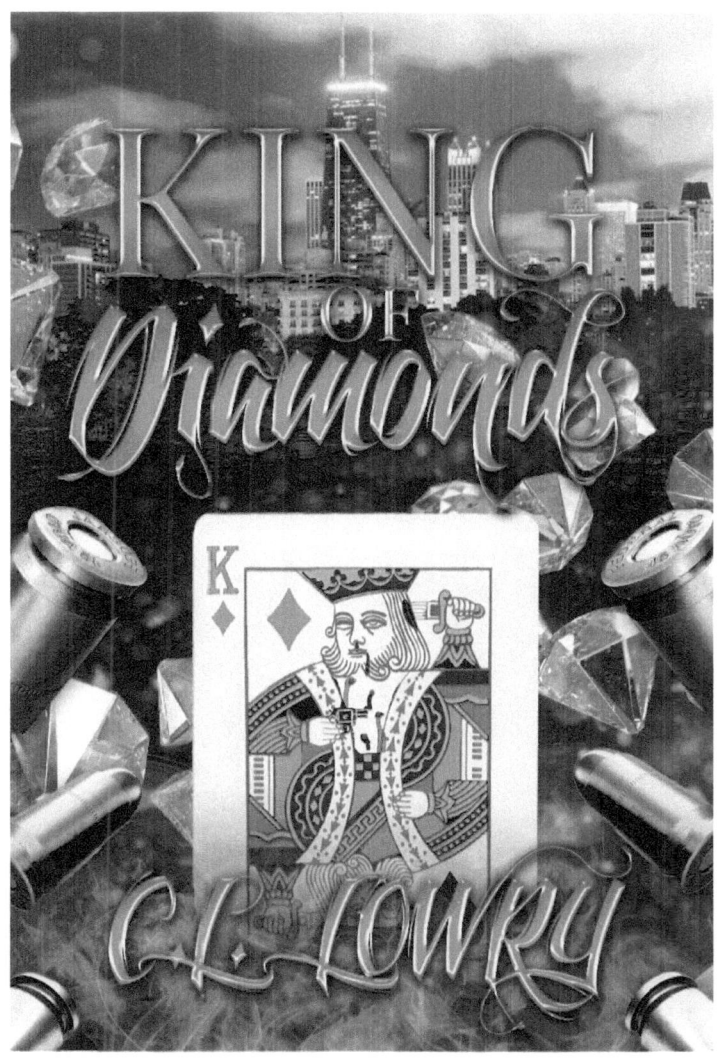

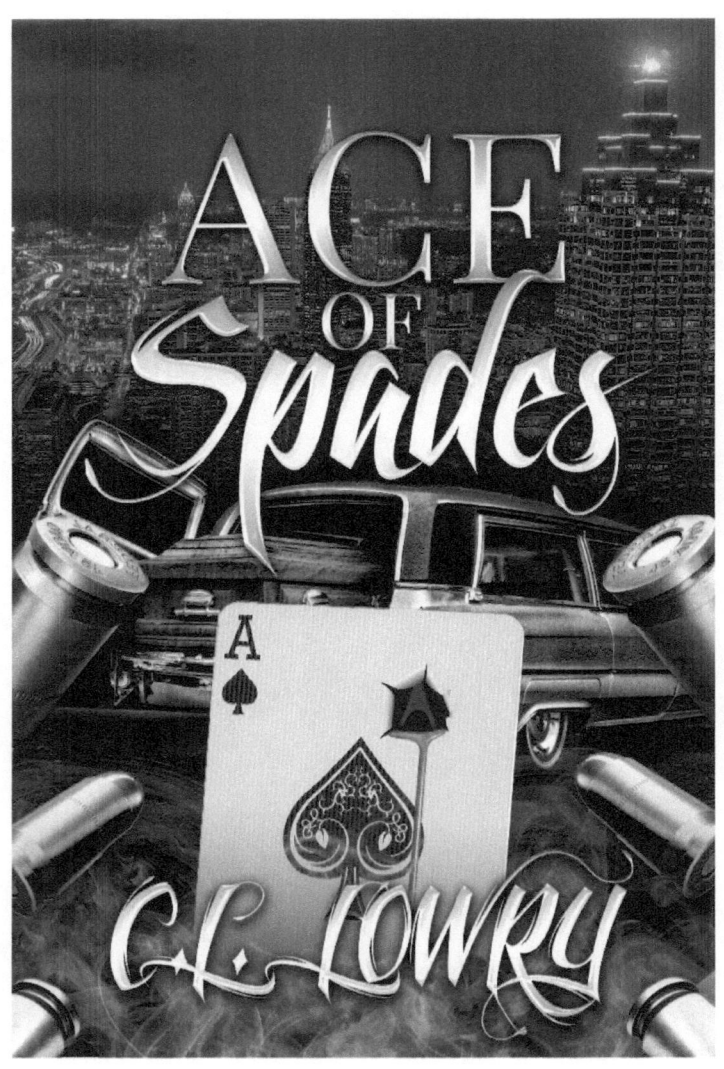

COMING SOON...

# ABOUT THE AUTHOR

**C.L. Lowry** is an award-winning author and filmmaker. Although he prides himself as being a prolific crime novelist, his pen game is versatile and allows him to navigate through multiple genres. Lowry was born and raised in Philadelphia, Pennsylvania but his family roots trace back to the beautiful island of Barbados, West Indies. Lowry uses his life experiences and creativity to demand his readers' attention with realistic scenarios throughout his stories.

When he isn't penning a page-turning novel, Lowry is behind the camera creating high-quality films under his production company, Black Lens Cinema. Lowry is also the host of the Fiction Addiction Podcast, where he interviews authors, filmmakers, and other creatives. Sign up for Lowry's spam-free newsletter to learn more about future releases, sneak peeks, special offers, and bonus content. Subscribers will also receive access to exclusive giveaways. To sign up, visit his website at **www.authorcllowry.com**.

# CREEDOM PUBLISHING COMPANY

Creedom Publishing is a fully incorporated publishing company. Much like our slogan "The Home of Creative Freedom," we are committed to providing new and upcoming authors with the resources and opportunity to share their creativity with the world.

Creedom Book Services is the parent company to Creedom Publishing Company. Under our publishing company, we provide quality books for readers of all ages. Whether it's the eye-catching childrens book series for young readers or the page-turning crime thrillers by award-winning author C.L. Lowry, every book under Creedom Publishing Company is worthy of being added to your library.

**Our books are available for purchase on our site and eBooks are available through Amazon Kindle.**